The Duke
of the Moors

A Regency Romance Novel

Audrey Ashwood

Print ISBN: 9781794670013

About this Novel

An ethereal beauty. A darkly handsome duke.
If she can't win his love, her family is doomed.

Yorkshire, Regency England. Miss Catherine Conolly is surprised by a mysterious invitation from a wealthy uncle who hasn't spoken to her in years.

Upon arriving at his formidable house on the Yorkshire Moors, she finds herself a pawn in his mischievous plan to gain influence over the enigmatic Duke of Rotherham – known as the *Duke of the Moors*. But enthralling as she finds the handsome man, his reputation and inscrutable manner are the subjects of much sinister speculation among the locals and the society crowd alike ...

As rumours swirl around the duke concerning the untimely death of his former love, Catherine considers abandoning her uncle's scheme. But how can she escape the man who's awakened a passion she never knew she was capable of?

Trapped between her family's pressure and the call of her heart, Catherine dedicates herself to sorting fanciful fiction from frightening fact.

Will she find love, or will the duke's dark past be her undoing?

Chapter 1

The carriage raced along the dark, wooded road, as Miss Catherine Elizabeth Conolly stared out the window, peering into the black, moonless night. Torchlight from the carriage illuminated figures on horseback in the darkness, who had appeared out of the shadows and who now threatened the coachman and groom.

"Catherine!" her mother shrieked with wide eyes, the sound of terror trembling in her voice. "Catherine! What is happening? Have we bolted? Have the horses gone wild?"

Catherine did not want to tell her mother the truth. It was too horrible to say it out loud, but she had no other choice. Her heart was beating wildly inside her chest, and she could barely breathe as she was overcome by fear – and regret.

"We should never have left so late in the day. I wish we had travelled at first light," Catherine said, as she tried to make sense of the scene that was playing out at breakneck speed outside. She held on as the carriage rumbled over rocks, and first veered dangerously and sharply in one direction and then another, as the coachman tried to elude capture. Gripping the seat, she wished they *had* bolted. Being inside an out-of-control carriage pulled by horses who were running free and wild, would be a preferable fate to what surely awaited her mother and herself.

"Can you see anything? It is so dark outside – there's no light. Have the torches been extinguished?"

"Mother, I do not know. There is one still lit, but I do not like what I can see in its light."

The carriage bounced, jolting both Catherine and her mother out of their seats.

Catherine gasped and her mother exclaimed, "Oh! We shall be dashed to pieces if we do not stop!"

"I would rather be dashed to bits and die mercifully, than meet the fate that awaits us..." Catherine crawled back onto the seat, a fearful expression on her face.

"What is it? What's out there?"

"Highwaymen. We are being attacked by highwaymen!"

"Lord preserve us!" her mother wailed as the carriage lurched, and then, suddenly, slowed down.

Catherine checked the latches on the doors. She wanted to be sure both doors were locked tightly. She dreaded what would happen if she and her mother were taken by the cutthroats she had seen on horseback. Her mother was shaking. Catherine fought the urge to weep, as her mother was doing, and tried to remain strong, but her fear was slowly overwhelming her. She jumped at every gruff voice that she heard from outside, and with every sound. She was panicked and as afraid as a field mouse being hunted by a cat.

Her mother cried and prayed, "Dear Lord, save us. Save us from these devils on the road. Protect my daughter that she may not be ravaged by these lowly criminals."

Catherine wrapped her arms tightly around her mother. She silently wished that these rogues would take what they wanted and leave her and her mother alone. She prayed for the coachman and the groom, not knowing if it wasn't already too late for them, after she heard pistol fire and saw a flash of light through the small narrow window of the carriage.

"Catherine! It is over for us – we shall be killed," her mother cried as she hid her face in the folds of Catherine's cloak.

Her breath was ragged, and Catherine could feel the stays of her corset digging into her skin every time she gulped for air. If the coachmen were dead – shot to death on the side of the road – what hope remained for her or her mother? What chance did two women stand against ruthless, desperate men?

To her horror, she saw a shadow approaching the windowpane. The latch rattled violently, and Catherine shrank back, willing her mother and herself to be invisible in the darkness. It was too late. A torch light shone through the thin pane of glass and illuminated her face, as her mother wept uncontrollably. Catherine looked away from the glare of the light, turning from its brightness.

"Get out of the coach!" a man demanded from the other side of the door.

Catherine heard her mother whisper. "Please, do not listen to him, we shall be killed if we leave the carriage."

Immobilised by the terror of their situation, Catherine sat frozen and unmoving as the latch rattled once again.

"I said get out! Do you hear me?" The man's voice was louder now. "Get out or I will rip this door off its hinges."

Catherine did not know what to do. She was paralysed by indecision and panic, and her mother hissed in her ear, "Do ... not ... open ... the door!"

The torch was removed, and she heard a sharp pounding on the thin carriage door, followed by the deep masculine voice saying: "Get out of this carriage, or I will shoot off the lock and drag you both out. You do not want me to do that, and it will not end well if I have to come in there and get you!"

"Catherine!"

"Mother, we do not have a choice, do we?"

The man pounded on the door again. Catherine trembled and her mother begged her, "Catherine, we are safe in here. *Please.*"

"No, Mother ... they have obviously learned that it is just you and me. We are not safe in here ... or out there," she said as the door strained against its hinges.

"I've lost my patience with you two fine ladies. This is your last chance. Come out of there, *now!*"

Catherine's voice came out thin and scared, in a nearly unrecognisable plea. "We're coming out – do not shoot us."

She reached for the latch, but her hand was shaking so badly that she could barely wrap her fingers around it. Her mother clawed at her, trying to pull her back into the seat. The door opened with a clicking sound that echoed throughout the stillness of the coach's interior. Catherine closed her eyes for an instant, as if she could will this moment to be over – for it to have merely been a terrible nightmare.

When she opened her eyes, she saw again that she was not asleep, and this was not a horrible dream.

A man stood outside, staring at her. His face was wrapped in black cloth. He wore a black hat and a mask across his eyes. Catherine forced herself to move and to step down out of the carriage. She was immediately struck by his manner. Instead of ripping her from the safety of the coach and flinging her to the cold, damp ground, he held his gloved hand out to her, offering his assistance as she stumbled, missing the last step.

"Careful," he growled, which seemed to Catherine to be a surprisingly chivalrous sentiment from a scoundrel.

In the torchlight, she saw the man's eyes glimmering. They were light, pale blue ... or were they grey? It was difficult to tell which. His eyes were narrowed into slits as he glared at her and said, "Tell the other one to come out and stand before us."

"Mother, do what he says," Catherine implored her, and she finally emerged from the coach. The older woman wept as she climbed down.

Catherine was astonished when her mother addressed the man directly. "What is the meaning of this? Do you intend to kill us ... to rob us? Do you know who you *dare* to attack? I am the wife of a baronet! How dare you commit this heinous deed against my daughter and myself," she shrieked.

"I beg you ... be quiet please, Mother," Catherine said in a low tone.

As Catherine's eyes adjusted to the dim light outside the coach, she saw that the man was not alone and that there were several others with him. The figures on horseback that she had seen, surrounded the carriage. The circumstances were as she feared, but she also saw that there were other men, dressed in livery, standing nearby. Her own men were alive! Relief flooded through Catherine's body. The groom was bleeding from his forehead, while the coachman was clutching his arm, but they were alive. They both knelt in the grass beside the road, a drawn pistol levelled at them by another man, who was wearing a black cloak, a black hat, and a mask.

There must have been four highwaymen, all attired similarly in dark clothes, and all masked. The man who had threatened to shoot the locks off the door of the carriage seemed to be their leader. Catherine reached for her mother.

"Do not listen to her, she is terrified. She does not know what she's saying," Catherine said to the man.

"Keep the old woman quiet, or you'll both regret it," he spat, as two of his men yanked the trunks from the back of the carriage.

Catherine watched as their clothes, their dresses, and their hats were thrown onto the ground in a heap. The men pawed at the dresses, making lascivious comments as they laughed. Catherine stared at the man who held the pistol that was aimed at her and her mother and tried to memorise any features she could discern. If she survived the night, she swore she would see this highwayman arrested and hung. Although she was not normally a violent or morbid person, Catherine was afraid for her life as she stood in the dark, with her arms around her mother. The terror that coursed through her veins, fuelled her thoughts of revenge, even if they were impotent and impossible.

"You keep eyeing me like that and I'll strike you. Look away, do you hear!" the man said in a menacing tone.

Catherine did as the man demanded, and turned away, but not before she noticed the strands of dark hair that had slipped out from under the brim of his hat. His hair was dark, maybe coal black, maybe a very dark brown – it was hard to tell in the torchlight. He was taller than her by a head, or maybe more. With her slender, small frame she looked like a young girl when compared to the bulk of his frame. She prayed that any detail she could recall would be the evidence a magistrate would need to send this man to the gallows.

A cold wind moaned eerily in the trees as Catherine held her mother closer. It cut through her cloak, chilling her to the bone. Shivering, she stood helpless as their belongings were dumped and left in the dirt of the road.

"They do not have anything worth our time," a masked man commented to his companion, who was kicking a trunk into pieces.

"There's nothing here! Nothing but ladies' clothes ... and who wants those?"

"Search the carriage!" the man, who was obviously the leader of the gang of highwaymen, roared to his men.

"There is not anything in there for you to take." Catherine's mother wept.

The men ransacked the coach, growing more and more frustrated. In the light of the torch, Catherine thought she saw the glint of a blade. When she heard the ripping sound of a seat cushion being torn apart by one of the men, she astonished herself by yelling out the word, "Stop!"

The man who had the pistol trained on her and her mother, turned to look at her. "Stop? You're not the one in charge here. Tell us where your jewels are hidden, and we will stop."

"We have none," Catherine replied.

"Two ladies travelling in a carriage with coachmen, who do not have valuables worth stealing? I think not. You are lying to me. You do not want to do that," the man hissed as he drew closer to Catherine, the pistol pointed at her chest.

"Leave us alone ... we have nothing for you to steal," her mother cried out.

"I think they're telling the truth. They have nothing," one of the men snarled from inside the coach.

"I bet ... they're wearing what they've got. We ought to search them." One of the men leered.

With the barrel of his pistol, the tall man eased back the edge of Catherine's cloak. "What have we here? A cross, is that all you have? You had better tell me where you're hiding all your fine jewellery, or I will let my men search you. You do not want that."

"Leave her alone!" Catherine's mother screamed as she unfastened her own necklace from her neck – a matching cross to Catherine's – and thrust it at the highwayman. "Take it! Take it! Because we do not have anything to give you. I wish I had a coffer full of jewellery to suit your greed, but I have nothing else."

Catherine's heart was beating loudly. In fact, so loudly that she was certain the echo of its beats was rumbling through the tress all around them. In the dark, and lit by the faint light, she stood with a pistol pointed towards her chest, while her mother, who was crazed with fear, suddenly became defiant in the face of unspeakable violence.

"We ought to take the horses and leave with them ... but we aren't a bunch of horse thieves, are we men?" the masked bandit said as he laughed in a deep baritone.

Catherine did not see any difference in what they were doing. Terrorising two women on the side of the road, was no worse than stealing horses.

"Who wants those nags?"

"Not us, not worth swinging for."

"What about the girl?"

"Leave her be. Come on men, there is nothing here."

"Sir, you mean, there is nothing for *us* tonight? Nothing for *our* trouble?" complained the man who was keeping his pistol aimed at the coachmen.

"They obviously have nothing worth taking," said the man Catherine thought to be their leader. "One's too old and the other's too ugly for my liking."

Just as Catherine's mother wanted to protest, Catherine nudged her swiftly to remind her to hold her tongue.

"Come on men, let's make for the road. We've wasted too much time and we have nothing to show for it." With a chuckle, he gave the ladies a wink and said, "I expect you to pay twice the fee of the highway, the next time you pass through my woods.... Understood? The wife of a baronet should be prepared to pay for her travels and her safety on the road."

The highwaymen left as quickly as they had come, disappearing into the night on their inky-dark steeds. Catherine's mother wept as she looked at the mess of their clothes, spread all over the road.

"Ruined! Look at all of my dresses! Trodden into the mud..."

Catherine rushed to help her servants as she listened to the sound of hoofbeats growing faint in the distance. Anger replaced her relief and she felt the sting of her impoverished state once more. How dare the highwaymen declare what she already knew to be true! They had nothing worth stealing – nothing at all. They did not even want their old horses. While she was trying to dismiss her anguish and fear, she felt only indignation, and she hoped that she would see the vile man who had dared to aim a pistol at her again.

However, the next time, she hoped she would be witnessing his execution.

Chapter 2

An hour later, the coachman and groom's wounds had been bandaged. The clothes had been gathered and packed into the remaining trunks and secured onto the back of the carriage. Catherine tucked her cloak over the ripped seats inside the coach. Stuffing from the seat cushions clung to her dress, and she unsuccessfully tried to brush it away. Her mother sat back quietly in the seat as the coach rumbled onwards.

But Catherine was not quiet – she was very nearly livid.

"How insulting to be treated like that at the hands of a common rogue!" she exclaimed.

"My dear child, you are *not* ugly." Her mother was obviously still smarting from the highwayman's insults.

"Oh, that is not what I meant."

"You are an exquisite beauty in your own right ... in fact, you remind me of myself in my youth. I was an ethereal beauty ... just as you are. However, truth to be told, you *were* white as a sheet."

"Well, if I recall correctly, I was not the only one terrified."

"We both still look like death, I am sure. The night has been hard enough. We should praise God we were delivered without further incident," her mother continued, "but I *do* wish they had not thrown our dresses into the road. I do not know if we will have anything that can be worn without cleaning and mending."

"Without further incident? Our clothes are filthy, we've lost a trunk, and the coachmen are injured! Oh, Mother. Was it really necessary to try to *impress* the men by letting him know your rank?" Catherine did not let her mother answer. "We can count ourselves lucky that we're still alive ... If only we had not set off from the inn so late in the day. Was it truly necessary for us to remain in our rooms in Helmsley for half of the day?"

"I was ill, and I could not bear travelling until I was better."

Catherine's mother, Lady Mary Conolly, was prone to dramatic turns and hysterics. She was also prone to illness, whenever she felt anxious. The lateness of their departure from the inn that day, was entirely because of Lady Conolly's poor health. A condition had come upon her suddenly, and Catherine suspected the ailment was the result of their impending meeting with the Viscount of Wharton. He was the reason why they were travelling in the wilds of the North Country. If the viscount had not sent a mysterious invitation to Lady Conolly, they would be safe at home by their own fireside and far away from the dangers of highwaymen on a dark country road in Yorkshire.

When Catherine thought about the invitation, she was fearful and furious in equal parts. Her uncle, a man she had seen infrequently, was a stern sort who never smiled nor uttered a word to her. She did not understand his wish to invite them to his residence, not after he had taken so little interest in his own nieces and nephew, until now.

"Mother, I still cannot understand why we must journey to Brigham Park? What could be there for us but humiliation? We are not of the same social standing as your brother. You witnessed it yourself – we did not even have anything that those terrible brigands wanted to steal from us!"

"We most certainly *are* of the same standing – even if my brother outranks us. You seem to have forgotten that your father was a baronet, and I am the sister of a viscount. We are worthy of being received in the house I once called home, and of being amongst genteel people and good society."

"I do not care for the society of Yorkshire or anything else I may find at Brigham Park. I want to go home. I want to turn around and go back to our own house. We would never have been in such danger if we had stayed in Cheshire. It is only here in this wicked, barbaric land that we have had to meet with such an ancient threat."

"My dear, it was by the grace of God we have not been harmed." Her mother looked at Catherine's concerned face. "We shall discuss the matter with my brother. He will want to hear of an attack such as this, and so close to his own lands. Perhaps something can be done."

"I pray that these lawless men are brought to swift justice, but I do not have the slightest faith that we will see that they are. I have heard of their crimes. They are rarely caught, even though I wish that I were wrong."

"Your uncle will see that they are found and brought to justice."

"It is the only reason I care to see him at all," Catherine said, as she sat with her arms crossed, warding off the chill of the autumn air.

"You must not say such things about him – he is family."

Catherine was undeterred. "I do not know why he sent us an invitation to visit him. It seems perfectly ridiculous that we accepted. I daren't imagine why he wished to include us amongst his acquaintances, when he has been noticeable only by absence these many years."

"Catherine, please. We are not in a position to reject his offer to visit. He is the wealthiest gentleman of our acquaintance. Do I have to remind you that we may need to seek his patronage? If you do not find his temperament or his manners to your liking, then I pray that you will remember that we may be forced to rely on his charity."

"Patronage or not, the whole situation seems strange. Neither of us know the reason why we have been invited. Are we so desperate that we are prepared to go racing across the countryside at the merest possibility of receiving charity from a well-meaning relation? Especially when that relation – your brother – has been absent from our lives, until the arrival of his invitation?"

Catherine's mother sniffed and dabbed at her eyes with a handkerchief before replying. "It was not his choice to be removed and distant from us. The distance to Cheshire is considerable, and he did have an estate to manage."

"Which, I remind you, remains unchanged. How many years has he sent nothing to you but the occasional letter? I cannot recall an invitation arriving for any other occasion. Neither can I recall him showing interest when we were in London, before Father died."

"You cannot blame my brother. It can hardly be wise for him to be seen in the same society as us. How else should he have behaved, considering the choice I made upon my marriage?"

Catherine sighed. Her mother was anxious but hid it well under a veneer of familial loyalty.

Catherine had no such loyalty to a man she had rarely met, and whom she recalled as being a terrifying figure in her youth. She remembered him as intimidating and imposing.

Catherine continued to stare apprehensively out of the window. She saw only the darkness of the night. When she could no longer make out the passing silhouettes of trees crowding the road, she was certain that they had entered the desolation of the moors. Shuddering, she recalled the landscape as a foreboding place in the day, but almost terrifying at night. The wind howled and moaned along the hilltops. The valleys were as comfortless as cemeteries, surrounded by grey rocks that resembled enormous gravestones. Marshes, which swallowed unwary beasts whole, were concealed as solid ground to the equally unwary walker. Caverns hid all manner of terrors. Crags threatened to crush an imprudent traveller – or concealed menacing cutthroats. Trees did not grow on the moors, leaving only dry grasses and brush for shelter. There was no cheer of cottages to offer warmth and protection. Instead, the loneliness was as relentless as the chilling wind that never stopped blowing in pitiable and ghostly cries that warned of danger. Inside the carriage, Catherine shivered again as she looked at the moors, while the wind whipped around the coach, its song a lament. Then, far away in the night, she thought she saw a faint light glowing high on a hillside, against a backdrop of utter darkness.

"We'll be arriving at Brigham Park soon. I do hope they have tea for my nerves, after what we have been through on this night," her mother said as she wiped her eyes.

Catherine wondered if the light she saw was Brigham Park. She prayed it was, as it stood at the end of their journey. She would be grateful when they managed to arrive safely. Yet, a part of her was filled with trepidation, as she wondered what could have caused her uncle to have so sudden a change of heart.

The coach rumbled on, and the light in the distance grew closer. Catherine's childhood memories of visiting Brigham Park returned, despite the many years that had passed since she had last seen the house. The residence, as she recalled, was like her uncle – old, cold and formidable. In the darkness, she would not see the contour of the great house where it sat alone on the moors, or its stone ramparts, but she felt its presence as they entered through the stone gates into the courtyard. She remembered, from her youth, that Brigham Park was a great fortress – a castle that brought back memories of stories of knights of old. It seemed to be just the sort of place where the land and forests would be filled with highwaymen. One might find ancient evils, such as dragons, Catherine mused, as the carriage slowed to a halt.

They had arrived at Brigham Park. They were safe and alive.

Chapter 3

Brigham Park was exactly as Catherine recalled from her childhood. The house was a foreboding place – drab and cold as the autumn weather outside. Tapestries hung from the walls, and all manner of weapons were displayed in readiness.

In the bedroom, which was to be hers for the duration of her visit, sat a large bed that was far more sumptuously adorned than any bed at her family's house in Winslow Court. However, despite the luxury of the room, she could not rest. The pillows were soft and the mattress better than any she had ever laid on in her life. The bed curtains were richly embroidered in flowers and vines that she would have found enchanting if she were anywhere else in the realm.

Still, she was haunted by a feeling she could not dismiss – of what might have happened to her and her mother in the woods that night. She thought of how close to death she had come when that scoundrel had dared to point his pistol at her. If he had wanted to end her life, he could have done so! There was nothing she or anyone else could have done about it. It was a moment she knew she would never forget, and arriving at her uncle's house, a place where she did not feel she belonged, did nothing to soothe her anxiousness.

The maid who had unpacked her clothes, promised to have something clean by the morning for her to wear to breakfast. The remainder of her dresses would be repaired and pressed, she was assured.

It was a kind and thoughtful gesture from a woman whom Catherine had just met.

As she lay in the near darkness – the only light from the fire in the hearth and the candle at her bedside – she wished for the comfort of her own room in Cheshire, small and plain as it was. She longed to see her brother, Henry, who was now the baronet. She wished to tell him of the horrors of her journey, and to hear his voice assuring her that all was well and not to worry. She missed her friend, Patience Smythe – the governess of her younger sister. *She* would understand the terror she had felt, Catherine knew she would. Lastly, she longed to embrace her younger sister Jane. Jane was a dear girl, who would be frightened by the tale of the highwaymen. Catherine would not tell Jane how close to death they had come. Rather, she would listen to Jane play the piano and admire her skill as she allowed herself to be cheered by the music.

She rose from her bed, and her feet felt how cold the floor was as she walked to the fireside. She could not sleep, and she missed her home and the people she loved. After a terrible evening, she wanted to be comforted by those she cared for, instead of having to lie in a bed that was not hers, in a castle she dreaded might be haunted.

Ghosts and other creatures roamed the halls of Brigham Park. These ghosts were fragments that she vaguely remembered from the stories her cousins, Denton and George, had told her when she was a child. Their old gore-filled tales did nothing to make her feel safe as she listened to the wind wailing in the chimney and working its way through the cracks in the window frame. Catherine shivered from the cold and from the fear of what fate might have befallen her. She wrapped her arms around herself as she sat by the fire and, finally, she wept – her body shaking from the emotions she had been too afraid to express to her mother. "For what reason?" she asked out loud, but she answered her own question in silence, *For my mother to come to beg my uncle for his support. To accept an invitation to this house that is grey, weathered, and severe in every way, just as its master is.*

She cried until she had no more tears left to weep. The anger she had felt earlier that evening returned. How was she supposed to treat her uncle, a man who did not care to acknowledge her or her brother and sister, while her poor dear father had lived? She returned to the grand bed as the fire died down and turned to embers. Tomorrow morning, she would meet her uncle. She was not looking forward to renewing his acquaintance, despite the desperation of her family's circumstances.

If her mother wished to beg for an allowance, then she should do so at once, thought Catherine, as she pulled the covers over her body and sank down into the softness of the mattress. Let her mother plead for charity, but Catherine would not. Catherine earnestly believed that she had a reasonable expectation to first know why she and her mother had risked their lives to come there.

When the sun finally rose, it sent faint rays of dawn light into her bedroom. She had not slept well that night. She remained in bed as the scullery maid relit the fire in the hearth, and she doubted that she would sleep for the entirety of her visit to Brigham Park.

After the maid had accomplished her duty and left, the fire warmed the room. Shortly afterwards, another maid appeared, announcing her presence with a soft rapping on the door. Catherine recognised her as the same woman from the previous evening. She was tall and sturdily built, and about a decade older than Catherine. Her demeanour seemed pleasant. Catherine found that she liked her at once, especially when she discovered that the maid had kept her word and had cleaned a dress that would be suitable for breakfast.

Catherine's mood brightened at the sight of the maid standing at the foot of her bed with the dress – a frock of cream with pink ribbon trim folded over her arm. The dress was plain by the dictates of fashion, but it was one of Catherine's favourites. It would be the dress she would wear when she met with her uncle.

She smiled at the woman. "Thank you for cleaning that dress. I am afraid the highwaymen made a terrible mess of things when they threw all of our clothes into the road last night."

"Miss, I heard about what happened to you. Did those men 'urt you?"

"No, I was unhurt. The coachmen bore the brunt of the attack."

"I wager they were brave, defending you from being killed?"

"Yes, they were courageous," Catherine answered as she thought about the injuries the men had sustained.

"It is not my place to tell tales and gossip, but I heard that His Lordship has ordered the doctor be brought to see to their wounds. I even heard that he paid the men for their bravery."

"The viscount?"

"Yes, Miss. I do not know if it's rightly true or not, but the word was spread this morning. I get scared just thinking about what lies past the walls of this house. Terrors like those keep me here at Brigham Park, where I belong. I would never venture out after the sun sets, not on the moors … People do go out on the moors, though … and sometimes they are never seen again. Haunts and ghosties, and all manner of beasts and evil spirits roam these lands. I have heard it said that any poor soul who dies on the moors is doomed to roam them without rest. There is a tale told around the fires in these parts. Would you like to hear it?"

"Yes, please." Catherine nodded.

"There was a woman who lost her child – a little girl. The child fell into the marshes one day, as she was picking wild flowers. They say she was searching for the prettiest flowers she could find, to place on the grave of her father. As she searched for the blooms, she slipped into the marshes, into dirt as thick as mud and as slippery as water … She drowned, the poor lamb. Her mother was driven to madness. She was seen walking onto the moors – it was late autumn – wearing naught but a thin dress. She had no shoes on her feet or shawl around her arms. They found her after a fortnight, frozen to death … However, even in death, she cannot find peace. She walks the moors searching for her child. On clear, dark nights the child can be heard wailing and crying and her mother weeping – doomed to wander the hills." The maid shook her head as though she was trying to rid herself of an unpleasant memory. "The dead do not rest on the moors – and neither do the living. I have heard it said that there are men who seek their fortunes robbing from the good."

"I cannot say anything about the ghosts that haunt the moors, but I know of the terrible deeds of the living men … It was dreadful, but I shall not think of it. I have other matters that require my attention."

"Yes, Miss, we should cheer ourselves by talking of other things. Would you like me to help you with your hair now? You have such thick, pretty hair. I would not mind if I had hair half as nice as yours."

"Would it be too much trouble?" Catherine asked the maid.

"Trouble? Dear me! I cannot remember the last time a guest of His Lordship asked me if I thought my duties were troublesome," the maid exclaimed.

"I apologise. I am not accustomed to being a guest of the viscount."

Catherine and the maid looked at each other. Catherine had the distinct feeling that the woman was appraising her worth, which she had to admit, must not be very much.

"What is your name?" Catherine asked. "If you like, we may dispense with formality. I am not a high-born lady." She smiled. "Well, I am sure you have come to that realisation from the state of my wardrobe."

"Miss, you are a guest here at Brigham Park. I will treat you as you deserve. But you may call me Bess, if that suits you."

"Yes, Bess, that suits me very well. I could use some help with my hair."

"Thank you, Miss. The housekeeper of the viscount has assigned me to be of assistance to you during your stay ... I've always wanted to be a proper ladies' maid and not just a housemaid," she said in happy excitement.

"Oh, I would like that very much. I am in need of a maid to see to my clothes and my hair."

Bess beamed and her dark eyes twinkled. "Thank you, Miss! And I do love me a bit of gossip … if you don't mind … even if I know it's against the good book to tell tales."

"It has been many years since I was here. I have no doubt that there are stories that only you know." Catherine smiled at the woman.

"Most certainly. It is not wrong to tell tales that are diverting. No, not when there's no harm to come from it."

"We won't tell a soul, will we? Now Bess, what do you think I should do with my hair today?"

"Don't you worry – I know just the thing."

Catherine settled into the tufted chair in front of a mirror. Bess happily arranged her hair while chatting about the comings and goings of Brigham Park. It seemed to be a good trade. Bess was allowed a respite from her work as a housemaid and Catherine gained an ally in the house. She felt buoyed by the new alliance. It was common knowledge that maids and footmen knew more about the family and their guests than anyone else did. Catherine knew that she could use a close friend, in a place such as Brigham Park, which was ruled by her uncle. Especially a friend who knew information that His Lordship might not be willing to share with her mother or her.

Chapter 4

An hour later, with her hair perfectly coiffed and pinned into place, and her dress immaculate and pressed, Catherine was ready to face her uncle. At least that was how she felt before she was invited to join him and her mother in his study.

When they descended the stairs, Catherine and her mother were warmly greeted by Denton, the viscount's son. He expressed his shock at their rude introduction to the moors and assured them all that was possible was being done to apprehend the rogues. He passed on greetings from his younger brother George who wouldn't be in Brigham Park for the hunting party, since he and his newly wedded wife travelled the continent for their honeymoon. Catherine was happy for her cousin, even though the news of his recent marriage surprised her, given that her uncle had not mentioned it in his letter. Denton led them to his father's study and, mindful of the viscount's impatient nature, soon excused himself with a warm smile and the promise to continue their conversation at a later time.

The viscount's private study was as she imagined it would be. The walls were of grey stone, panelled with dark, carved Tudor wood. Tall arched windows let in light, and an enormous number of books and ledgers were neatly arranged on dark-wooded shelves, behind glass doors.

Catherine found it odd that her uncle should meet with her and her mother in the study, where one would expect him to conduct business, and not in the drawing room where he would receive his guests.

The viscount smiled as he took his place behind an enormous oak desk, like a king on his throne. His eyes were cold, despite the faint upturned position of his lips.

"Please be seated," he said, before Lady Conolly and Catherine settled themselves into high-backed chairs. They were quiet in response – neither of them saying a word.

Catherine was not sure if she should refer to the man in front of her as Uncle or as Lord Wharton. Calling him *Uncle* assumed a certain degree of familiarity that she did not feel. Sitting straight in the chair, she did not think she would ever be able to relax in his presence. He was tall, with a thin frame, and his face was long and gaunt. His hair was as grey as the stone of the walls. His complexion had the same leaden cast to it, as if he rarely saw sunlight. By comparison, Lady Conolly appeared not to be related to the viscount in any way, with her chestnut hair – the same shade as her daughter, although with a few more strands of grey.

"I thought we might meet in the drawing room, where we may have tea. Or in Mother's old sitting room." Lady Conolly began the conversation.

"The drawing room would not have been an ideal place for our discussion. I have guests arriving today. They have no interest in the business between us, sister."

Lady Conolly nodded her head.

"Denton is seeing to the guests while we become reacquainted," he added calmly when he noticed the surprised look on his sister's face. Then he was silent again.

Catherine waited for one of them to speak, to dispel the tense quietness that had descended upon them. She was struck by the absence of any closeness or affection between them. When she was with her brother Henry, they laughed often and played jokes on each other. Or, at least, that was how she recalled them behaving before her father had died. Her brother rarely laughed these days. Now, his brow was nearly always furrowed with worry. Catherine missed the carefree days, but she was grateful that she had had them. At the moment, the serious look on her uncle's face told her that he and his sister had never shared any days that were filled with laughter.

"What business do we have between us?" Lady Conolly started the conversation again, trying to sound optimistic. "And what of your guests?"

"My guests are the very reason I have invited you here," explained the viscount, "but first, let us speak about the unfortunate incident that happened during your journey. I have called for the magistrate to come at once, but I do not know what can be done. Yorkshire is a place like no other county in England. The people are far more superstitious, and the highwaymen are audacious. Regrettably, they are seldom brought to justice."

"The attack occurred near your land. Surely something can be done?" Lady Conolly exclaimed.

"If it were that simple, I would have been rid of the menace of these thieves in my district long ago. They move by night and are unrecognisable because of their masks. Also, they never strike in a predictable manner. It is a source of embarrassment to me that they operate along the road leading to Brigham Park. I have posted men from time to time, but the highwaymen then operate along other roads – they are as unpredictable as the weather." Lord Wharton paused shortly. "That is of little importance, however. What is vital is that neither of you were hurt. As to your men, I have seen to them. They will be compensated for their bravery and your carriage will be repaired while you are here, enjoying the company of my guests and the hospitality of this house." He glanced at Catherine.

Lady Conolly's disappointment was barely concealed for a moment. She replied hesitantly, "I presumed from your invitation that you wished to meet with me to hear about our living arrangements now that my poor husband is no longer with us"–she looked at him in bewilderment–"or something of that nature – now that I am a widow. I was not expecting to be amongst guests for any length of time, aside from an occasional dinner."

"An allowance?" the viscount replied. "Is that why you think you came here? To see me about a living?"

The lady's cheeks burned red with what Catherine could only guess was embarrassment. She watched as her mother attempted to regain her composure. "Brother, what possible *other* reason could you have had for sending an invitation for a visit? You are surely aware that when my husband died, he left us in a great deal of debt. We are nearly penniless." Her voice almost shrieked.

"Yet you arrived with two men?"

"They have been in our employ for years ... they are loyal and necessary. I may do without the required number of maids and footmen, but not without a coachman and a groom," Lady Conolly answered indignantly.

"Sister, let us rather speak about matters not related to your present financial concerns. I assure you, we will address those in good time. This morning, I wish to talk with you about the hunting party that will be arriving today and tomorrow."

"Hunting party?" Catherine asked, despite her years of training not to speak first to a person of superior rank.

"That is the reason I invited you." Lord Wharton turned his attention to her.

She felt his gaze, which was cold and merciless. He was as intimidating as she remembered him to be, were it not for something that seemed to resemble ... was it a smile?

"You invited us to a hunting party?" Lady Conolly jumped in. "Would my son not have been a more appropriate guest than my daughter?"

A hunting party did not sound like a social occasion that would mean very much to Catherine. If it were in her own county, where she and her family were widely known, she might have enjoyed the dinners, parlour games, and teas that accompanied a hunting party. Yet, here in Yorkshire, her only connections were her uncle and cousin. What delight could be had in a drawing room filled with people who greatly outranked her?

"Your son has business that requires his attention. *His* future is assured." Lord Wharton spoke to his sister, then turned back to address Catherine. "I have it on your mother's word that you are not engaged."

"I am not engaged," Catherine answered quietly. She was not expecting her uncle to concern himself regarding her prospects.

"Nor will you be without the proper introductions to gentlemen of rank and worth," he continued.

"I am not sure I understand," Lady Conolly said as she stared at her brother with an expression of confusion.

"With the death of your husband, your situation has become, dare I say, precarious," the Viscount explained. "I would like to offer you my assistance as it concerns my niece. It is my wish to invite you to my home, so that you may meet with gentlemen who are wealthy and well-connected. I could not extend an invitation before your mourning was at an end."

Lady Conolly nodded. "You wish to offer your assistance in finding a husband for my daughter?"

"Assist? I do not know if I would use that word, but I do wish to provide her with every opportunity to meet suitable gentleman who may elevate her rank and your family's financial situation – through marriage."

Catherine abhorred being spoken of as if she was not present, but she had no other choice but to sit quietly. She listened to her uncle and her mother speaking about her prospects. Finally, her uncle looked in her direction.

With his cold expressionless features set, as if in stone, he said, "There are several young men who will be arriving to enjoy the fine hunting the season offers. I have one such gentleman in mind, who would be an excellent choice for a young woman with your attributes. I believe His Grace would be an ideal match for you."

"A duke? For my daughter? Oh, brother, you have given us a gift!" Lady Conolly replied excitedly.

Catherine was speechless. Her question about the true nature of the viscount's invitation had been answered, but she was even more confused than she had been before.

Her uncle, a man she had never viewed in the role of a benefactor, looked at her directly, as he continued. "I have not taken a role in your patronage until now. Under my guidance, I will see that you choose carefully. There will be many men amongst the party who are eligible, respectable and wealthy. His Grace would be the first amongst his peers for connection and rank, although I dare say, you would do well with any of the guests."

"Catherine, you have never been introduced to a duke. We do not count one amongst our own company." Her mother beamed with happiness.

"Thank you," Catherine replied, uncertain of anything else to say. She was nervous about being introduced to a man vastly higher in position than herself or anyone that she had ever met, for that matter. However, that was not the sole cause of her apprehension. How could she ever hope to capture his attention?

"Mother? Why would a duke, who could marry a beautiful countess, or the daughter of a marquis, ever consider a match with a woman without a title?"

"Do not concern yourself with trivial matters such as a dowry and finances, child. They are best left in the hands of gentlemen. You may not be aware, as you have been in mourning for some time and not amongst society, but you have succeeded in cultivating a reputation as a fine woman and a beauty. I heard it remarked upon by more than one of my acquaintances while I was in London in the spring."

"Me? You must be mistaken," she said. "I am not a beauty. In fact, only a short time ago, I was called the opposite."

"Nonsense." Her mother could not help but interject.

"I am a woman, like any other," Catherine said to her uncle. "I am in possession of the usual accomplishments with little else to recommend me."

A real smile formed on his lips for the first time since the conversation had begun. It was a sight that seemed to surprise both Catherine and her mother. It vanished as quickly as it had appeared. The viscount then shrugged his shoulders. "Think what you wish, but gentlemen have different views on such matters. I would not be astonished to find that you are the most handsome woman in attendance during my hunting party."

"What of her dresses and clothes?" Lady Conolly asked quickly. "Will she be fashionable and stylish compared to your other guests? "Beauty cannot overcome the economy of her and my own wardrobe."

"Your wardrobes are adequate. Amongst my guests, you may not be adorned as royalty – but Catherine, you will be the toast of Brigham Park, and you may rely on it."

Catherine was not sure whether she knew how to be the toast of any place. The time she had spent in London, which was her first season, had ended abruptly with the sudden illness of her father. She had missed her second season, and now at one and twenty years of age, she was neither impressively elegant, nor stylish. Despite her rosy complexion and shiny curls, she felt truly comfortable only amongst the society of Cheshire. Reflecting on the manner with which her uncle had assumed to speak to her, as a kind patron, she considered his comments to be rather wondersome. In fact, Catherine longed to ask someone about the transformation she now saw in her uncle's attitude towards her. She was not prepared to believe that he was suddenly so altered that he could dismiss years of not acknowledging her or her family. It seemed equally unbelievable that he would wish to invite her and her mother to associate freely amongst his connections and to see that she was well-matched. The whole affair was curious, but Catherine felt she did not have the luxury of dwelling on her uncertainty.

"Catherine." Lord Wharton said her name sharply, waking her from where she had drifted away to in her thoughts. "What is your decision? Will you consider making the acquaintance of His Grace, the Duke of Rotherham?"

Lady Conolly was enthusiastically nodding her head for yes. She quickly grabbed her daughter's hand, but Catherine hesitated in her reply. She recalled the name Rotherham, as a fleeting memory. She had heard it before, of that she was certain. The title *Duke of Rotherham* was familiar, but for a strange reason. Was he not known as the *Duke of the Moors*? Why was he so associated with the dreary treeless hills? Was His Grace as dark, brooding and dangerous as the landscape?

Feeling her mother and uncle watching her, as they waited for her response, Catherine answered, "I would be honoured to meet His Grace."

"Then we are in agreement. Our business is concluded."

Chapter 5

"His Grace arrived with a valet, three trunks filled with clothes, his own horses for hunting ... and a carriage ... and a phaeton ... and two teams. I heard he even supplied his own brandy." Bess's words echoed in Catherine's mind as she entered the drawing room before dinner.

She was dressed in a gown of cream satin with a delicate ivory sarsenet drape from the bodice to the floor. She wondered if her dress would not be out of place amongst the other ladies. Walking into the drawing room of Brigham Park was an experience like no other. She tried not to stare at the vast collection of oil paintings or to stop to examine the deep crimson cushions of the couches and chairs, which were embroidered in a crewel pattern that complemented the rugs under her feet. The room was a testament to the line of Wharton – a room carefully decorated during centuries long past. It displayed the Whartons' wealth and their long history of influence and power, with careful curation.

Even if she had wished to examine every cushion, or sought to study the paintings, she was not given the opportunity. Her mother rushed to her side and immediately reached for Catherine's arm, to steer her towards her uncle.

"My dear, you have arrived late," her voice sounded tense, "but I do not mind. The duke has just come downstairs to join us. As you may observe, there are many gentlemen who may be suitable for your hand. But none have his background or wealth."

Catherine glanced around the room nervously. She saw several gentlemen of different ages, some accompanied by ladies and others grouped together, chatting as they waited for dinner to be announced. The men were dressed in their dinner finery of polished boots, black coats, and white cravats. The ladies were dressed as if they had just arrived from London. In a sea of silk turbans, peacock feathers, and satins of every colour, Catherine tried not to feel conspicuous in her simple, but still pretty gown of cream with a matching ribbon entwined in her chestnut curls.

"Mother, I am afraid I am not dressed to meet a man of the duke's rank."

"You may be poor, but never forget you are half a Keeling. Hold your head high, as you always do, and remember that compared to the other women in the room, you are the comeliest of them all. You have no need for any artifice or contrivance to be a beauty."

"Which one is *he*?" Catherine whispered to her mother as she glanced quickly and inconspicuously around the drawing room.

"Your uncle tells me the duke is that gentleman standing beside the Earl of Burwickshire – the shorter man with light hair," her mother said as they approached Lord Wharton. "I may not introduce you, as I have not yet had the honour of being introduced myself, but your uncle will undoubtedly wish to present you to His Grace."

Catherine sighed. She was crestfallen. Two men were standing side by side near the card tables – one was tall, lean, and muscular and the other was, as her mother described, short and in possession of fair hair, lighter than summer wheat. They were surrounded by women who laughed gaily at every word uttered by the two gentlemen. If His Grace the Duke of Rotherham was the shorter gentleman, Catherine had to admit that his height, as well as his round figure and face did not resemble the man she might have dreamed of marrying some day when she was younger. But in the end, it did not matter how her future husband looked, as long as he treated her and her family well.

"There is my niece ... making her appearance in the drawing room ... at last! I feared you were not well," Lord Wharton said to her with a friendly tone, but there was the typical coldness in his eyes. He acknowledged his sister with a simple nod.

"I am well. Please forgive the lateness of my arrival. I became temporarily lost in this great house," she said, thinking silently that this was not entirely a lie. Brigham Park *was* enormous – a vast house that rose from an old keep, or fortress, and became a grand residence, which branched out in nearly every direction. While Catherine had not been lost this time, it was entirely possible that she may become lost in the foreseeable future.

"That is entirely understandable," the viscount said. "It can be confusing for a visitor. I have been told as much on many occasions. You are here now, I am pleased to say. I believe there is ample time to make the necessary introductions to the Duke of Rotherham before we go through to the dining room."

"Thank you," Catherine replied.

With a reassuring pat on her arm, her mother urged, "You go with your uncle – he will see that you and His Grace are acquainted. In the meanwhile, I will speak to Lady Ellsworth – I have not seen her for a great many years. I wish to know how she fares."

Catherine swallowed. She felt anxious at the very thought of making the duke's acquaintance. What would she say to such a man? What would he say to her? She was aware that she was barely regarded as gentry, and at just above a knight in rank, was considered by many above her to be almost a commoner. What would a duke think of her presumption in meeting him, even if Catherine would feel more confident in her approach if she were to be introduced to the less attractive of them both?

"Come along," Lord Wharton said to Catherine. "You will find His Grace to be an engaging man. I dare say, he has the command of the room."

Catherine knew her uncle was correct in his assessment of the gentleman's popularity. Not only were women gathered around the duke and the earl, but other men, and quite a few of the ladies, surreptitiously glanced towards him, leaning in to listen or stare in awe of him. He was clearly well received. Dukes were not as commonplace as the other titled nobility. The inclusion of one on the guest list of the party was quite a compliment to her uncle.

Lord Wharton's stride was larger than her own, as he moved quickly and purposely across the drawing room. Catherine walked faster in an effort to match his pace, so that she did not appear to be following behind him as a servant might follow a master. As they approached the duke, the earl, and their bevy of admirers, she suddenly felt terribly aware that her dress seemed unfit for the occasion in its simplicity, after all. She felt even plainer when she drew near to the ladies whose ears dripped priceless jewels and whose necks were wrapped in pearls.

"Now, now ... do keep up," Lord Wharton said to her under his breath as they approached the small gathering of stylish women and titled gentlemen.

At that moment, the usually strong young woman wished she was not being forced to meet His Grace. Catherine would have liked nothing better than to dash away from the drawing room and to run back up the stairs to pack her clothes. This introduction had the obvious appearance of artifice, which caused her to chafe quietly under the influence of her mother and her uncle. If there were so many eligible gentlemen amongst the guests, why did her uncle not introduce her to any other of them, rather than singling out the one gentleman of the highest rank? She was blushing by the time she stood before him.

Curtsying as she was presented, she was mildly startled that the man she had thought to be the duke, the short, corpulent fair gentleman, was the earl. His companion – the taller man – was His Grace.

Every pair of eyes in the drawing room was trained on her, but the eyes that mattered most belonged to the duke. His gaze was direct, and his eyes were the colour of the sword blades on display in the great hall, or perhaps a summer storm on the horizon. They were grey and did not appear to have a speck of warmth in them, and neither did his first words to her.

"It is an honour to make your acquaintance, Miss Conolly," he said without a single indication that he welcomed the introduction.

A hush had fallen on the crowd that surrounded him. The duke was of greater than average height. He towered over her by a head or more. His figure was well-proportioned and muscled. His hands were sinewy – evidence of a great many hours spent on the saddle. She found herself drawn to the lines of his figure and his manly shoulders, broad from outdoor pursuits. His jaw was blunt but handsome, and his features were refined in a masculine manner. He appeared an Adonis come to life – a statue of a Greek warrior, with dazzling grey eyes and lustrous dark hair. When he spoke to the company that surrounded him, his voice was deep, and his laugh was pleasing and baritone. The silence was only interrupted by the soft whispers of the ladies, as Catherine felt compelled to continue the conversation after her uncle excused himself and walked away.

"Your Grace, do you enjoy hunting?" Catherine asked, feeling her cheeks blaze with colour.

"Hunting? I do not care for the sport, but I enjoy riding across the moors."

"I take great joy in the hours that I spend riding. It is amongst my favourite pursuits," Catherine responded, pleased that she had discovered a subject in common with the gentleman.

"I have brought a pair of Irish stallions, solely for that purpose. They are the fastest in the North country, I am proud to say," he answered in a tone that suggested his enthusiasm was for his horses and not the pleasure of speaking with her regarding their shared interest.

"My father will not ride a horse that is not of Arabian descent," a woman said, attempting to capture the duke's attention with her smile and her comment.

"Arabian?" the duke asked. "Lady Francis, you must be referring to the Moorish blood line that runs in the horses in the South?"

As she was without knowledge of racing horses, Catherine felt as though this topic had been a horrid error of judgement. How on earth was she supposed to match wits with a man who enjoyed a recreation she could never afford and, what made matters worse, who did not seem to be interested in her? Feeling foolish, she considered excusing herself from the conversation and the presence of the duke, all the while looking around for an ally.

Then she noticed the shorter gentleman with pale skin and hair to match, the earl, and he was smiling at her.

Chapter 6

The Earl of Burwickshire was far more receptive to Catherine than the duke. The earl was a genial, jovial sort of gentleman who seemed to have a natural tendency to make everyone around him feel at ease. Catherine was grateful that while His Grace seemed to be ignoring her, the earl initiated a conversation with her in the drawing room after dinner. Her mother, who in her youth had been known in this county, seemed perfectly at home amongst some of the older women. She had once called many of them her friends, before she had married beneath her station, and she was happy in their company now.

Catherine felt alone and without a friend to cheer her, or anyone to talk to. She was watching the crowd, hoping to find someone she could befriend, when she was approached by the earl. At his side was a young woman who looked nearly identical to him in height (and roundness) except that her blonde curls were pinned high on her head. Her round breasts and those same curls bounced whenever she walked or laughed. Her generous bosom was encased in an exquisite and voluminous blue gown that Catherine imagined must have cost a small fortune.

"Miss Conolly, perhaps you do not recall meeting me before our brief introduction earlier," the earl said pleasantly. "We were introduced in London some time ago."

Catherine curtsied, as she smiled in response. "Lord Burwick-shire, I apologise, but I do not recall meeting you before tonight. It has been a long time since I was in London."

"I am often forgotten ... I have that way about me," he responded brightly as if the fact that she did not recall him did not bother him in the slightest.

Catherine was attempting to think of something nice to say in response, when the young woman, who was of her own age, abruptly added her thoughts to the conversation. "You are the same Miss Conolly whom *I* remember seeing in London! You were quite the sensation ... and then you disappeared! How mysterious ... Everyone wondered where you were last season," the woman said cheerfully as she looked at Catherine.

"My disappearance was not as mysterious as you may imagine, I am afraid. My family was in mourning and could not attend the season."

"My apologies," Lord Burwickshire chimed in. "Miss Conolly, allow me to introduce you to my sister, Lady Frederica Grantley."

Catherine bobbed down again in a curtsy. "Lady Frederica, it is a pleasure to meet you."

"Oh, the pleasure is mine. You must forgive me for speaking as I did about your disappearance," Lady Frederica said, obviously stricken. "I did not know that it was due to such a terrible tragedy."

Catherine was moved by the sympathy of this young woman. She expressed her feelings as readily and easily as her brother, both of whom were the epitomes of kindness in a drawing room filled with seemingly wealthy people.

Catherine smiled at Lady Frederica and replied in a soothing tone of voice, "Lady Frederica, there is no need to forgive you ... you could not have known about my circumstances, which are far better now that I am here in your amiable company."

The young woman glanced at her brother and then back at Catherine. She began to beam once more, her face plump, dimpled and beautiful. "That is so good of you to say so! I am pleased ... no, that is not the right word ... I am *delighted* to make your acquaintance. I wished to meet you when you were last in London, but there was not an opportunity. But, if I may be honest, I had hoped your departure from society was due to some great scandalous love, or perhaps an elopement to Gretna Green." She laughed.

"Frederica! How you do talk – you must not say such things!" her brother chided her in a teasingly sweet way that Catherine immediately found charming. "Miss Conolly has only just made your acquaintance. She does not know of your love for those ridiculous novels you go on about."

"I do not mind. I find novels to be entertaining reading," Catherine replied cheerfully.

"You do?! Then we have that in common, do we not?" the young woman answered happily as her curls bounced up and down energetically. "How wonderful!"

"Frederica ... Miss Conolly. It appears that my presence is being summoned for cards. If you ladies will excuse me," the Earl of Burwickshire announced and gave a mild gesture with his head to the back of the room.

Catherine turned her head. She was surprised to see the Duke of Rotherham looking in her direction. For a moment, she wondered if he was looking at her. She very nearly smiled at him, acknowledging him, when she realised, to her embarrassment, that he was not looking at her. He was subtly gesturing to Lord Burwickshire.

"The duke does not like to be kept waiting. Apparently apart from him, I am the only man in attendance who has the kind of purse that can support the large wagers he prefers," Lord Burwickshire said with a grin and a shrug.

"Take care not to lose too terribly," Lady Frederica said quickly, "Good luck, brother. I hope you win every hand you play!"

"So do I!" Catherine added with a sincere smile. "Good fortune to you, Lord Burwickshire."

"Ladies." Frederica's brother bowed and then turned to join the duke for cards.

"Oh, that duke, that Rotherham, he is a devil when it comes to cards, but you can never discount my brother entirely. Do not mistake my meaning, my brother is courteous to a fault. He is always willing to permit others to win, *if* it suits him. But he does possess considerable skill when he chooses to make good use of it. If he so wished, he could make a living as a card shark! I know it is perfectly indecent to say such things, since we have only just been introduced, but it is the truth, even if it *is* shocking," Lady Frederica said to Catherine and both of them laughed.

"You cannot shock or astound me, so have no concern that you might."

"I am glad to hear you say as much. I have been told by my brother that I am far too opinionated for a lady. What do you think? Can a lady be too opinionated?"

"Oh, absolutely not!" Catherine replied. "I do not see why a woman should not express her opinions as freely as any gentleman, considering she takes care not to give offence or offer insult."

"Then you do understand me – how delightful! I find that not many of my friends truly do. I say what I please, which most women do not."

With Lady Frederica so obviously cheered at the idea that she had found an ally, and Catherine thrilled that she was in such pleasant company, she proceeded to make an inquiry she would not have dared to, before knowing Lady Frederica to be so free with her opinions. "You mentioned that His Grace enjoys gambling. What else do you know of him?"

"There is not much to tell about him, I am sad to say," Lady Frederica whispered. "I pride myself on knowing something about everyone. I like to think of myself as knowledgeable of the news around town when I am there, but I must confess that I know very little of that gentleman. What little I do know of him comes from vague rumours and from what I have learned from my brother, who has met the duke at clubs and at many card tables. Rotherham, I have heard, keeps to himself and is not overly fond of society, which may account for my lack of knowledge of his habits, aside from gambling."

"It is a wonder that he should appear at the house of my uncle for a hunting party..."

"It *is* a wonder, is it not? They call him the Duke of the Moors – an inauspicious title. There is a tale, a tragic one, that came to my ears. He once loved a woman. His regard for her was strong and true. Although little is known about the woman, her fate is steeped in mystery. It has been suggested that he was the cause of it – perhaps a quarrel that was never resolved. Some say she fled from his house, riding into the dark of the night, during a terrible storm. But who knows? I have heard it said that she disappeared and was never seen again. He was a different person before the tragic event, or so I have been told. Oh, it is such a shame."

"What of his family? Do they share his woeful reputation?"

"If they do," Lady Frederica whispered, "I do not know it. He is the last of his lineage. His brother died young, years ago. His father and mother, they are all departed from this world."

Catherine stood silent, contemplating all she had gleaned from her new friend. The duke was proving to be even more enigmatic and interesting than she had first assumed, surrounded by rumours of a lost love and a tragic family history.

"The moors are steeped in tragedy," Lady Frederica continued with her voice back to normal, "but the woods on the edge of them are frightful. The trees are filled with all manner of desperate men. I am astounded that any of our party arrived here safely with those horrid highwaymen lurking about. I was told that you and your mother were attacked by those savage men. How thrilling a story that must have been! I say that because you were unharmed, or else I should not say it was thrilling at all."

"I am not sure if I would call what happened that night thrilling." Catherine had a flash of a memory of the highwayman who was in charge – the tall man, the one who pointed a pistol at her chest.

Lady Frederica covered her mouth as she made a small, nearly imperceptible noise, that sounded like a squeak, and then she leaned in so close that her soft breasts pressed into Catherine. Her eyes shone brightly as she whispered, "When I heard about it, I thought that the whole event sounded as if it could have come from one of my novels. A dark, stormy rainy night. Men on horseback, and a dashing rake of a fellow who wishes to kidnap you for *ransom*. What a story that would be! Was that how it happened?"

Whether the rake was dashing or hideous, Catherine did not know. All she knew was that he had glimmering eyes, dark hair and a nasty, terrifying voice that made her tremble in fear. Seeing her companion staring at her with wide-eyed wonderment, like a child waiting for a story, she dismissed the memory, but could not help but be amused at Lady Frederica's romantic vision.

"It was not raining. I am sorry to disappoint you. I do not recall if any of the men were dashing, as they were all swathed in black," she said as she watched her mother swiftly cross the drawing room towards her to interrupt the conversation the two young women were having.

"Your uncle wonders why you are not watching the card game with the other ladies, as the duke seems to be playing a fine hand," Lady Conolly chided her daughter.

"If he is winning, that means my brother is not doing very well," Lady Frederica exclaimed. "I should go to his side at once. He may need me to comfort him if he loses. If you will excuse me."

With Lady Frederica swiftly away to the card tables on the opposite side of the room, Catherine was left in the presence of her mother, who did not appear to be very happy. Using her fan as a shield for her face and her mouth as she spoke, her mother whispered behind it, "Why are *you* not at the duke's side, wishing him good luck?"

"I was not invited to be at his side."

"Nonsense! Are you going to wait for an invitation to join the other ladies who have surrounded him? How will you ever win his attention if you do not show your interest?"

"He barely acknowledged me when we were introduced. I am convinced that he has no opinion of me."

"Catherine, you must be mistaken. Your uncle told me that the duke was quite taken by your beauty. He demands that you go to the card table. This instant."

Catherine stared at her mother, unsure of what she had heard. "My uncle demands that I go?"

"I am sure that he saw what I, myself, observed, that you were busily chatting with a young woman when you could have been spending your time in better pursuits. Stop being silly and obstinate and go, your uncle insists – and so do I," her mother hissed behind the façade of the fan.

Catherine had no choice but to oblige. Walking across the drawing room, she felt the intense glare of her uncle. A glance in his direction quickly confirmed his displeasure of her actions. Finding a place near the card tables, Catherine stood close to Lady Frederica. Surrounded by the presence of the other women, and some of the men who were watching the game with interest, Catherine had the distinct feeling that there was another reason she had been invited to the hunting party. While she might never ride on the back of a swift horse in pursuit of prey, it did not mean that she was not on the hunt. She eyed the duke with a growing sense of resentment and understood that he was the prey whom her uncle wanted her to pursue. She looked up and caught her uncle's eye once more. He was staring at her, his face set in a frown. Why did her uncle insist that she chase the duke, when there were so many eligible young men in the drawing room? A connection to the family of the Earl of Burwickshire would undoubtedly be desirable, thought Catherine. However, as she did not catch the Duke of Rotherham's notice for even a single second, she was left to wonder about her uncle's true intentions. What was it about the duke, besides his rank, that warranted all of this effort?

It was a question she knew needed an answer – and soon.

Chapter 7

Catherine's curiosity concerning her uncle's interest in her future did not subside the following day, nor the day after. The Viscount of Wharton made his disapproval of her failed attempts with the duke known to her through a series of scowls. He occasionally sent her mother to remind her that she was to do all that was right and proper to attract the attention of the duke. Catherine began to grow tired of the entire enterprise, as she was beginning to feel cheapened by it – and increasingly fatigued and frustrated. She speculated about her uncle's true motives, and for that matter, those of her own mother. In fact, her uncle's actions, and his growing dissatisfaction with her, began to make her more and more suspicious.

But after two days, she was no closer to discovering his intentions beyond suddenly wishing to become her benefactor.

To top it off, the duke seemed to be resistant to her every effort. He excused himself whenever she joined his group, he ignored her when she spoke, and he did not look at her in the adoring manner in which the other men of high rank did. Catherine did not like to think it was true, as her mother was quick to assure her, she was not amongst the lowest ranked women in beauty at the party. She was even told by her new friend, Lady Frederica and the maid, Bess, that she was the envy of many of the young ladies for her thick chestnut hair and her porcelain complexion.

It was the third day of the party when Catherine stood in the drawing room, late in the afternoon. Lady Frederica was not always available to be her companion, as the Lady was quite popular, as was her brother, regardless of his claim to the contrary. Without their company, Catherine was left alone with a book (which she was never able to continue reading). Her mother refused to let her have a moment's rest from the task that involved the Duke of Rotherham.

Faced with this dilemma, she found herself caught in the throes of a dull decision. Should she have tea with a sandwich, or tea with a tart? That was all she had for amusement. The hunting was over for the day, and the men were enjoying the other women's company while refreshments were served. Catherine watched the duke laugh and flirt. If it was true that she was the comeliest of the ladies' present, then why did he not acknowledge her?

Catherine searched the room for a distraction, and saw her mother eating bite after bite of cake in the company of an older pair of women. Lady Frederica and her brother were engaged in a rousing game of whist with two other guests. Away from the card games and the throngs of people gathered around the tea and sandwiches, she suddenly spotted her cousin, Denton Keeling, just as he was exiting the drawing room.

Catherine felt an impulse to follow him. Denton seemed to be set on a path for the library, the study, or the stables, but she doubted she would have the opportunity to speak to him alone, again, unless she seized it. Catherine doubted that anyone would miss her company, so she rushed as swiftly and discreetly as she dared, to join him in the hall.

"Cousin." Her voice was soft a she reached his side, and she noted his astonishment at seeing her there.

"Catherine? You almost scared me with your sudden appearance, as if you were an apparition!" he said in his good-natured manner. "I have not spoken to you all day."

Denton was the heir to the title of Viscount of Wharton. He was an even-tempered man, a model of decorum who resembled his father in looks but did not share the same icy character. Catherine liked her cousin Denton. He had a way about him that had always made her feel comfortable in his presence, despite their vast difference in rank and wealth. Unlike her younger brother Henry, who was not at the party, Denton had always seemed very amiable. Catherine hoped that the amity he felt towards her, or familial loyalty, would give rise to candour. She looked over her shoulder. Catherine was expecting her mother or her uncle to come out of the drawing room on their heels. She did not have to try very hard to imagine the scene that might ensue. She would be ordered back into the drawing room to continue her increasingly desperate attempts to capture the duke's attention.

With a deep breath, she focused on her cousin instead, as she looked up to him and said, "I did not wish to appear like an apparition, but I would like to speak to you."

His eyes searched hers, and she saw his expression change from one of greeting to curiosity. "Catherine, you look pale. Are you unwell? Is that why you wished to speak to me? Do you require an apothecary or a doctor?"

"Yes ... I mean, no. I was not aware I looked ill. If I do, it is undoubtedly because I have not had a moment's rest since I arrived here," she said as she pulled him aside into a quiet alcove of the great hall.

"Whatever can it be? Is the room not to your liking? Are you overwrought because of the terrible incident that befell your party on the road? Tell me, and I will do all of which I am capable to see that whatever may be the cause of your unrest, it be corrected."

As she glanced over his shoulder and around him, again, she was certain she must have appeared furtive. Here she was, as nervous as a rabbit, waiting for a hawk to swoop in and make a meal of her. In truth, she did not wish to be interrupted nor did she wish to have anyone overhear her conversation with her cousin.

"I wonder if I may speak to you of a more private matter?" she asked. "I do not want to interrupt you from your errand, whatever it may be, but I do not know when I will find another time to discuss this matter with you."

"What matter would that be?"

"I do not wish to say," she whispered covertly, "not in the company of others."

"Is it a secret? One you wish to share with me? I was on my way to the stables to see to the horses for the hunt tomorrow ... but ... well, I do not think anyone will overhear our conversation if you would join me in my mother's old sitting room. Do you care to join me?"

Catherine nodded and then followed her cousin through a house that was equal parts castle and equal parts labyrinth. They arrived at a pleasant, but small room that was located not far from the library.

The room did not seem to belong at Brigham Park. Its walls, floors, and furniture were clothed in whites, greens, and pale pinks, and the sitting room reminded her of a spring day, or a stroll along a garden path. Everything inside the tiny room was covered in floral designs, and flowers and green vines danced along cushions, pillows and the rugs. She knew this small sitting room had been the favourite room of the late viscountess and also of her own mother.

"I do not wish to delay your duties as a host ... I know that planning the hunt requires a great deal of effort," Catherine said, not mentioning her anxiousness concerning her fear that her mother might come bursting in. "Thank you for speaking with me."

Denton sat down on a tufted chair and beckoned for her to sit across from him, which she did. Catherine looked over her shoulder one last time. There were no footmen, no maids, or staff in this room, and no other guests. With a sigh of relief, Catherine knew that she had better say what she wished to say and be done with it.

"I do not wish to cause offence to either you or your father. The invitation to attend this party, and your treatment of me and my mother has been without fault," Catherine said, wishing there was some other way to say what she wanted without seeming disloyal, but there was no other way.

"Please go on, dear cousin."

With a long deep breath, Catherine plunged ahead, aware that she might not be able to retract any of the sentiments she might utter. "Cousin, I do not understand what your father's motives are concerning his role as my benefactor. Can you tell me what you know?"

"Perhaps I did not understand you correctly. Did you say that my father has taken on the role of your benefactor?"

"That is true. He told me and my mother this after we arrived. He explained that this was the reason why he invited us here after we had completed the period of mourning for my father. He wished to provide me with an opportunity to meet eligible young men."

"Oh?" Denton Keeling looked confused.

"However, since my arrival, he has appeared to wish that I only seek the attention of one gentleman in particular, even though there are a number of suitable, unmarried men in company."

"Whom might that one gentleman be, if I may ask?"

"The Duke of Rotherham."

"The duke? Are you certain you are not mistaken?"

Catherine smiled at his question. "I am quite certain. At every opportunity, I am to be in the company of His Grace. Can you account for such a strange request?" She paused. "Cousin, can you know what your father's true motive is, for this strange invitation and subsequent request?"

Catherine watched as her cousin sat back in his chair, his brow furrowed – not in anger, but he appeared to be puzzled. That look lasted for a brief moment, before he rose abruptly to his feet. "If my father has decided that Rotherham would be a suitable match for you, then who am I to question his judgement?"

"I am not questioning his judgement, not at all. I just wish I understood why he insists that the duke is the *only* match for me. Cousin, do be reasonable. We both know that I have little to offer a man of his rank. I bring no dowry. I have no lands and properties to offer him on our marriage. What connection can be gained by a marriage to me, the daughter of a baronet? Now, do you understand why I wished to speak to you? I do not wish to anger your father. Not now, when my family is dependent on his and your generosity. If I knew the reason – if I only knew why he insists I pursue a man who does not care to pay me even the tiniest speck of attention, then I would be content to do as your father has asked."

Denton was looking down at his feet as she spoke. She realised far too late that she may have spoken entirely out of turn, but it was also too late to remedy the issue. The viscount may be stern and his intentions impossible to discern, but Denton was his son, after all.

"I can offer you nothing but speculation, and that will not answer your questions." He spoke in almost a whisper. "I would suggest that you speak to my father, even though I know all too well how imposing he can be, especially when he is entertaining a house filled with important guests."

"I hope I have not offended you, cousin," she hazarded.

"You have questions … you are inquisitive and intelligent. That hardly constitutes an insult. No, cousin, there is no offence taken."

"Tell me, do you have any thoughts on the matter? I do not care if they be false. I am keen to hear any thought at all that you may share with me?" she said as she stood from her chair.

"Nothing I would share, and nothing of any consequence." He did not meet her gaze.

Catherine examined her cousin closely. He was no longer at ease. Tension had settled into his shoulders and onto his face. She could see it in his stance and the expression he wore. He was hiding something from her, but what was it? Perhaps it had no meaning for her situation, but she was not convinced. Her uncle clearly had a motive for his actions. She did not believe him to be a kindly old relation who suddenly wished to make amends to a niece he had ignored for the better part of her life.

As she followed him out of the sitting room, she wondered how she could discover the truth without her cousin's help, or indeed the assistance of anyone else.

Chapter 8

Catherine's conversation with her cousin was immediately followed by a stern but whispered reproach from her mother. Just as Catherine attempted to join the circle of people around the duke, he made an excuse to retire before the company in the drawing room made their way upstairs to dress for dinner. To her astonishment, however, he did not appear in the drawing room before dinner. He did not sit at the enormous table in the dining room, and he did not reappear afterwards. Catherine wondered if she was the cause. She overheard Lady Frederica telling her brother that she had heard that His Grace was enjoying his own company after his brisk ride earlier in the day. She thought of the maid Bess's report that he had brought his own brandy with him to Brigham Park. He may, she speculated, be upstairs in the comfort of his rooms, sitting beside the fire, sipping brandy and reading a book – or at least, that was how she imagined him.

As strange as his disappearance was, and it was duly noted, his company was not required for the other guests to enjoy their amusements after dinner. So, Catherine began to regard the duke's absence as a curiosity and little else. With him gone, vanished somewhere into the house, neither her uncle nor her mother paid her any attention. For that evening, she was left at liberty to enjoy the amusements of the drawing room without having to endure the boorish behaviour of His Grace.

At the end of the evening, Catherine retired to her room anticipating a restful night's sleep, but that was not to be. Long after the sounds of the other guests making their way to their rooms had passed her door, she lay in bed awake. She stared up at the canopy high over her head. Her thoughts were unsettled, even after a brief respite from her impossible task of securing the duke's attention. She thought of her cousin's discomfort as she had pressed him about his father's motives for inviting her to the party. He had reacted with surprise at her confession that it was the Duke of Rotherham her uncle wished her to engage in conversation. Why was her cousin so uneasy by the discussion that he suddenly, as she believed, wished to escape from her company?

Then she pondered the matter of the duke. She knew him to be capable of laughter, of harmless drawing room flirtation and of conversation. She had observed him with the other women of the party. Why did he react so strongly and so adversely to her and not to a single other woman in the same manner? He barely concealed his contempt for her, which made her uncle's request to pursue him even more perplexing.

She thought of Bess, the maid. Perhaps Catherine could ask her what her master's motives might be, but she doubted such a line of inquiry would prove to be beneficial, and it would be considered odd to say the least, given their positions. However, any answer she might give, be it false or true, could be more information than Catherine had been able to gain from the conversation with her cousin. Tomorrow, she would try to discover what she could, but she would have to tread carefully so as not to appear disloyal to her uncle.

With a plan in her mind, a plan she had no real hopes would

bring a successful result, she was left to speculate about the duke. He was a good-looking man, there was no doubt of that. She ascertained from his posture and the way he spoke, that he was a gentleman in command of great wealth and influence. What harm would it do for him to acknowledge her occasionally, rather than treat her to his cool, distant stare? She had not wronged him in any way, however, he acted as if he perceived her to be responsible for some unknown and wicked deed. What was that? She had done nothing but speak to him and attempt to engage him in polite conversation, while trying to remain pleasant in his presence. What wrong could he imagine had been implied in those actions? What slight or what insult?

As she became more agitated by her thoughts of the duke, Catherine found herself unable to rest any longer. She threw back the cover and rose from her bed. She could not quiet her mind enough to allow rest to come to her, no matter how weary she might have been. If she did not find a way to rest, she knew she may very well become ill – something she had already been asked about that very day. After such a disappointing party, she had no wish to become ill at her uncle's house, so far away from the warm welcome of her own bed.

Perhaps, she decided, if she could read for some time, she may find a way to distract herself from all the thoughts that kept her awake. She considered the book that she had brought with her, packed in her trunk. It was from her father's library. He loved books, but he did not have the necessary wealth to amass a great collection. After his death, most of the volumes that remained had been sold in an effort to raise money for other more important expenses. The precious few books that were not sold, were well-read, slightly worn, and Catherine had almost memorised them all. She knew that she would not find the distraction she sought in that book. She decided to venture to her uncle's library to borrow a book or two. A story she did not know would offer her some respite from the chaos of her thoughts. *Yes*, she said to herself, a new adventure was what she required – one that was to be found in the pages of an unread book.

Catherine opened the door of her room and peered out into the dimly lit corridor. She was met with silence. The quiet was not punctuated by laughter wafting upstairs from the drawing room, nor the faint sounds of voices from other rooms, as it had been all day. The quiet was complete. No one was awake. Catherine slowly closed the door again, mindful of any squeaks from the hinges. She dressed quickly in an afternoon dress, which she decided was far better than her nightgown and robe, and hastily pinned her hair in a haphazard bun. It would not matter how she looked, for no one was awake to see her. However, Catherine did not wish to be found in a state of undress with her hair around her shoulders, should her uncle be awake somewhere in the house, or if she hazarded upon a footman who was posted as a sentry.

With a candle in hand, Catherine made her way out of her room, slowly. She was careful not to make a sound. She had no desire to be found out of bed and out of her room at that late hour. If her reputation was besmirched, her chances of ever being married would vanish as quickly as the duke had that afternoon. She winced. Why was she thinking of him again? The purpose of this risky enterprise was to distract herself from all thoughts of *him*. If she was willing to risk her reputation, which was truly all she possessed in this world, then she did not wish to think about him for another infuriating second. Quietly, she tiptoed down the grand staircase, taking care to move as swiftly as she dared. In the candlelight, the house was still a dark, dreary place. Catherine could well imagine that it was haunted. After she reached the base of the stairs, she walked through the great hall, stopping just long enough to listen to the sound of the wind in the chimney of the immense stone fireplace.

The sound was as eerie as any of the spectres she imagined were lurking in the shadows beyond the light of her candle, and the few remaining candles lit in sconces along the walls. Standing perfectly still, she tried not to think of the chilling moans of the wind as it whipped around the house and wailed down the chimney through the fireplace. Catherine was heartened by an image she had of her mother, who would probably have fainted at such a fright. As ghostly as the house was with its gloom and frightful noises, she was not prepared to return to her room unsuccessful. She would not be deterred from the lure of the library by any of the ghosts that might be lurking about.

She held her candle out in front of her to light the way ahead and sped as quickly as she could to the library. She did not see any footmen, or anyone who might witness her late-night adventure. She was hoping that she would be safely back in her own bed soon, and no one would ever be any the wiser. She found the door of the library unlocked and slipped inside, closing the door behind her. She was immediately awed by the room that was more cavernous and larger than many others in Brigham Park. In fact, the faint light of her candle did little to dispel the immense darkness inside the library. As she stepped further in, she noticed a fire remained lit inside the hearth, although it was apparent that it would soon die. Drawing close to the dying embers of the fire, she warmed herself after the cold walk through the house. Catherine shivered, not only from the cold. She tried not to think of how many generations of people had lived and died in this house, and how many of their spirits might still be haunting it.

She quickly dismissed her thoughts as silly and childish and left the fireplace to set about the task at hand. She began to search through the thousands of books in the viscount's collection with determination. With so many volumes, it was easy to become lost in choosing a book. The library contained all the expected works of literature and history. There were scores of atlases, as well as books detailing the local flora and fauna of Yorkshire. She found books of legends, of epic medieval sagas, and poetry. Catherine was not certain how much time she had spent perusing the collection, before settling on a *History of Yorkshire* and a novel by a famous Scotsman, whose work she adored. With the books in one hand and her candle in the other, she left the library.

Just as she entered the great hall, she heard the unmistakable sound of footsteps on the stone floor of the house. To her horror, they were approaching her position. Somebody was awake and was nearby! Quickly, she blew out the candle and slipped into the shadow of a doorway. She carefully opened the door to the drawing room close by and heard the hinges squeak. The shrill sound echoed into the quiet of the dark hall, announcing to whomever may be approaching, that she was right there in the drawing room.

The footsteps became louder. They did not slow or falter, as they might, had the person responsible for making them, heard the creaking of the hinge. Concealed behind the door, Catherine peered through the narrow crack, attempting to see the person who was boldly parading around the house without a care of being caught.

Surely, she thought to herself, *it must be a footman or some other member of the staff, either working late, or perhaps awake at this early hour.* Her heart thumped inside her chest and she willed herself not to make a sound. Her breathing was loud to her ears, and came in great gasps, so she forced herself to hold her breath as the unknown person came closer and closer. The footsteps were loud, almost as loud as her own breathing and her pounding heartbeat. She assumed it was a man because of the loudness of the steps, but she could not be certain.

From her vantage point, she could see the great hall and the staircase leading to the second floor of the house. She hoped that she would not be discovered by whomever happened to be walking around the house at that hour. How would she explain that she had snuck downstairs to the library? It was the truth – but who would believe such a boring truth? Especially when it was far more interesting to suppose that she was snooping around ... or ... meeting someone. She dreaded to think of what would be said were she discovered, and she wished whomever was about would hurry along to their destination.

Catherine strained her eyes in the dim light and saw a shadow at the same moment as the footsteps became so loud, that she was certain the person must only be a short distance from her. Should she close the door and wait for a few minutes to avoid detection? No, the hinges would surely give her away.

She stared and waited impatiently as the shadow grew larger and larger, and the steps became louder and louder.

Then she saw the person.

It ... it ... was ... the highwayman!

He had come to Brigham Park!

She shrank back in terror. The highwayman had infiltrated the house and found her. She expected to see the black mask, and to hear the voice of the highwayman in her ears, but she realised she was mistaken. It was not the highwayman.

To her astonishment, the mysterious person was the Duke of Rotherham.

Catherine could scarcely believe her own eyes. His Grace, who had disappeared from the drawing room that afternoon and who had not come down for tea or dinner, was now walking up the stairs in the middle of the night. As far as she could tell, from her hiding place, he was dressed for riding, from his boots to his coat. She blinked a few times as she tried to make sense of the image.

Studying the gentleman, she wondered if she was in error. Could it be someone else? Did she only *think* she was seeing Rotherham?

No, she was not mistaken. The tall man she was surreptitiously watching, *was* the duke. She *knew* it was him, by his confident swagger, his gait, and the arrogant way he carried himself.

In amazement, she asked herself why he would be out riding well after midnight. Her mind was reeling, but suddenly, another dilemma sprang to her mind. If the duke was out of his room and so was she, would it be assumed that she and the duke may have arranged an illicit meeting? It was preposterous to her to think of it. In truth, she knew that anyone who had seen them together would know that it was quite impossible, but still, the danger for potentially scurrilous gossip lurked. Wouldn't that be interesting for the wagging tongues

— a scandal about a duke and a lowly baronet's daughter found together late at night? Oh, her reputation would be ruined! She must not allow herself to be discovered.

When she was certain that the duke had climbed the stairs and was far down the corridor, she left the safety of her dark hiding place. She dared not light her candle again until she was closer to her room. The darkness and shadows would offer her some protection, she concluded, as she walked silently across the great hall and up the first flight of stairs without making a sound. She was beginning to feel confident of her chances of returning to her room undetected, as she reached the landing of the grand staircase.

If her candle had been lit, she might have seen the shadow move, and may have detected the alteration in the gloom's density, but she did not – until it was far too late.

With a gasp that could have become a scream if she had not caught the sound in her own throat, she saw a tall, broad-shouldered figure approaching her swiftly on the landing.

She closed her eyes as fear overwhelmed her, and she nearly stepped backwards down the flight of stairs. She was stopped from falling to her death by a gloved hand wrapped around her arm. The grip of the man's fingers tightened to keep her from losing her balance. Catherine opened her eyes. The man who was keeping her from tumbling backwards down the stairs, and who had appeared from the shadows like a ghost, was the Duke of Rotherham. His hand gripped her arm firmly, and he drew her away from the edge of the steps so that she could regain her footing on the landing.

Catherine looked down at her own hands. She was astounded that she had not lost her grip on her books and candle. She reasoned that her nearly fatal fall had happened so quickly that there had been no time for her to react. If the duke had not caught her, she would have fallen and broken her neck. As relieved as she was, she also felt anger welling up within her. If he had not terrified her by hiding in the darkness on the landing, she might not have lost her footing in the first place!

Her heart was beating loudly, and her pulse raced. She heard the rush of blood in her ears. Catherine tried to lean against the railing to regain her composure, but the duke would not permit it. Pulling her back towards the shadows, he hissed into her ear, "Are you trying to be seen? Do you wish to be found?"

"No, I do not," she replied as quietly as she could, while she wrenched her arm out of his grip. "However, I wonder the same about you!"

"What are you doing following me about at this hour?" he asked in a low, menacing tone.

"Following you? Have you not observed the books in my hand? I was not following you! I was searching for something to read!"

"At this time of night? With an unlit candle? Do you think I am a fool?"

"I would have you believe it, because it is the truth!"

"If you insist on telling me such a wondersome story, do not presume I would believe your falsehood–"

"I came upon you by happenstance and nothing more." Catherine interrupted. "I was not following you, nor did I wish to. Why would

I? For what reason?"

"There can be no reason, none suitable for such an insult. I knew I was not alone … which is why I waited on the landing for you. I could have allowed you to fall but I did not. Now I want honest answers to my questions."

"I owe you no such debt, Your Grace," Catherine hissed. "If *you* had not been acting like a thief, and prowling the house after dark, I would not have witnessed your return from whatever errand I dare not venture to guess. If *you* had not been out at such an hour, I would not have observed you. If *your* presence was not concealed on the landing, you would not have surprised me on the staircase … and I would not have been nearly killed." She kept her voice as near to a whisper as she could manage in her rage.

"What were you doing out of your bedchamber, if you were not spying on me?" he demanded.

"I have told you the answer already, but you will not listen. I was in the library, searching for books to occupy my time. I was unable to sleep," she answered, and almost wanted to add *because of you,* but she shut her mouth as he examined the books in her hand.

"A History of Yorkshire?" he asked as he peered at the gold-embossed cover of one of her books in the dim light. "What does a woman, such as you, care about the history of this region?"

"A woman such as *me*?" she responded with disgust. "How you insult me, Your Grace!"

"Do you continue to deny that someone has sent you to discover my whereabouts this night?"

Catherine's resentment for a man who treated her as if she was beneath even his scorn, bubbled to the surface. "I *did* notice your absence at dinner, but rather than venture from my room to discover the reason for it, I rejoiced in it. If it were to reoccur, I would not miss you at dinner tomorrow or the night after that. You may stay gone as long as you please and keep whatever hours you choose. If you enjoy riding on the moors in the dark of night, then do so. Know this to be true, that I have no interest in following you, nor was I entrusted with such a dubious task."

With that said, Catherine was ready to walk off. Just as she turned to leave, he drew close to her. Catherine could feel the heat from his body radiating through his clothes. She became aware of the scent that filled the space between them. It was an intermingling of a faint trace of her own rose water perfume and his masculine clean sweat. As she waited for him to respond to her impertinent remark, she looked into his face – at his eyes, which were impossible to see clearly in the darkness. She only saw an angry glimmer that shone directly towards her.

Until that moment, she had not been fully aware of how large and imposing a man he truly was. Rotherham was big, muscular, and did not intend to give her room to leave. His hand fit completely around her arm, while Catherine stood close to him waiting for him to say something to her. A few more seconds passed. Then, he drew even closer to her as he said in a tone that implied he was not to be disobeyed. "I have no more time to waste with you. The hour is late, and I am tired. You have seen nothing this night. Do you understand?"

"Sir, how can *I* tell anyone that I have seen you at this hour as it would also reveal that I, too, was not where I should be? My reputation would never recover from the scandalous talk that would circulate. Rest assured, I will not say anything about you or the odd hours you keep – not because you have commanded me into silence, but for my own self-preservation."

"See that you keep your silence."

"If *you* remain silent–"

"Take your leave of me. I tire of this conversation." With that, he let go of her arm and stepped back.

Catherine wished she was not in such a compromising position, or she would have said several things to him (and loudly, too!) that would have made her earlier impertinence seem trivial. How dare he dismiss her as if she were a servant! Yet, she did not wish to tarry on the landing any longer. Every second she spent in his presence, was one more second where she might be discovered with him.

As she closed the door to her room, Catherine rubbed her arm where he had squeezed it. She lit her candle again and changed back into her nightgown.

Catherine decided that his reputation would not be ruined by any escapade, so clearly, he must be protecting someone – or why else would he have been so threatening? A ridiculous thought crossed her mind. *Was it possible that the duke and the highwayman were the same person?* She dismissed the thought as quickly as she had had it. It was far more likely that his secret was a romance that he wished to keep far from prying eyes. If she knew for certain, that he *was* meeting a woman from the hunting party at late hours, Catherine would have given the evidence to her uncle in private. Then, he would realise that his insistence on her pursuit of the duke was in vain.

Snuggling under the covers, she opened the *History of Yorkshire* and thought of the duke's dismissal of her choice of reading material. If he was romantically involved with a woman, then he would not have been receptive to Catherine's attempts to capture his attention. Smiling at the realisation that she was not the cause of his disdain, and that he was clearly being loyal to someone else, she began to read the first chapter.

However, no matter how engrossing the book she read might have been, she was haunted by the incident on the road, and the chance encounter with the duke. As the wind howled outside the windows of her room, another memory of the highwayman came to her. How odd, she thought to herself, that His Grace evoked such a strong reaction from her that, for a moment, she honestly thought he must be the highwayman. It was perfectly ridiculous, she decided, but as she pulled the covers higher around her, she wondered if such an idea was as silly as it seemed. She tried once more to concentrate on the book in her hands, to chase the memory of her conversation with the duke out of her mind, but she was unsuccessful.

For a moment, her reading was supplanted by gnawing doubt and fear, but then she dismissed those unsettling thoughts by reading page after page of the *History of Yorkshire* – until the faint light of dawn filtered into her room.

As the sun rose, she was finally able to find sleep.

Chapter 9

"The highwaymen struck again last night, Miss Catherine. Is that not dreadful news?" Bess wakened Catherine with the latest gossip from the servants' hall, as Catherine was still yawning and attempting to make sense of what had happened to her last night. Her candle had burned down to a stub in its holder and the books, stacked neatly on the bedside table, were proof that her excursion downstairs had been real and not a dream.

"Did you hear me? Miss? You look terribly tired. Did you not rest?"

Catherine blinked a few times, rubbed her face with her hand and felt her arm.

"Poor lamb. Here, drink your tea while I lay out something nice for you to wear."

Catherine's arm was still sore from where His Grace had grabbed her to keep her from falling backwards down the stairs. If she removed her nightgown, she suspected she would find bruises on her arm from a man who had been lurking in the shadows like a criminal, or a thief.

Catherine stared at Bess, and the full realisation of what the woman was chatting about dawned on her. She jumped to her feet and joined the maid. "Bess, stop fretting over my dress. Did you say that there was another attack by the highwaymen? Last night? Are you absolutely certain?"

Bess nodded her head as she answered, "I am sure of it, Miss. It's all anyone can talk about this morning – anyone downstairs that is. It's a dreadful business, if you ask me. It frightens me to think on it. Do not be worried, however, you are safe here in this house. Have your tea, and I will see that you look as pretty as a blossom when I'm finished with you."

Catherine was trembling. A strong cup of tea might calm her nerves, but what of the racing thoughts in her head? She silently vowed not to try to allow her imagination to get the better of her. As she lifted the teacup with an unsteady hand, she was careful not to spill a drop. The Duke of Rotherham *was* the highwayman after all!

"Miss, why, bless my soul, you're as pale as a ghost. Should I send for a doctor?" Bess asked, a look of concern in her eyes.

"Bess, I have not taken ill, although I fear I may well do so if I do not rest."

"Miss?" the maid said as she stared at Catherine, concern still present in her eyes.

"Bess, I do look dreadful, I am sure of it. I have not rested. However, that is not my concern at the moment. Put my dresses down and tell me all that you know about the attack that occurred last night."

"Oh, it's the highwaymen, isn't it? I keep forgetting that you were nearly murdered by them. I should not have mentioned what happened to you. I should not have said a word about it," Bess said, and she looked as pale and stricken as she declared Catherine to be. "I am sorry, Miss, you poor dear! What was I thinking? It's little wonder to me that you're not sleeping. If *I* was attacked by a highwayman, I should never sleep again!"

Catherine smiled at the woman, to reassure her, as she said, "Please have no worries."

"By the grace of God, you are unharmed, but I should not talk about that scoundrel – not to you," Bess replied.

"No, Bess, on the contrary. I want you to tell me all that you know about him. Tell me what happened last night, and what you have heard. You will not make me fearful."

"I will do as you ask, but if it was me, I would not want to hear a single word about that awful man!" Bess declared.

Catherine felt a temporary pang of guilt for not being open with the kind maid, but she could not reveal her burgeoning opinion about the matter, which, while it was surprising to her, would be shocking to Bess.

Catherine hoped that she did not appear to the maid to be anything other than mildly interested in hearing about the highwayman in such detail. "My interest in the subject is one of curiosity, I suppose. I wish to see the criminal brought to justice. I want to hear every detail of any of his actions, no matter how small or unimportant. Only then will I be able to find peace."

"I also pray he is caught, Miss Catherine. I pray he has his day on the gallows! What man would make his living doing the devil's own work?"

"Bess, I agree. Now calm down. Come over here, sit down and tell me all that you know. Even the gossip."

A glimmer of guileful joy crossed Bess's features. "Yes, Miss. I do not want to disappoint you. But I better keep to my duties while I speak to you. I will tell all that I know. However, I do not know much, if the truth be told."

"Very well, Bess. I will content myself to drinking my tea. Leave nothing out of your tale," Catherine said as she sat on the tufted ottoman at her dressing table.

"The highwaymen attacked some unfortunate travellers last night. I heard that this morning. Those people were robbed of their jewels and their money."

"Was anyone injured?"

"I do not think so, or else I would have heard about it."

"The travellers, do you know who they were?"

"No, Miss, I don't ... Just a pair of unlucky souls, unknown to me. They say they were rich as kings, however."

"Do you know at what hour the attack occurred? And where?"

"No, unfortunately I don't know much else. I just heard the story at breakfast. One of the lads who work for the stable master, was passing through the village early this morning and he heard about it. If I hear more of the story, I will be sure to tell it."

Catherine thought about the duke and his mysterious errand. Where had he gone? What she had first decided must have been a romantic tryst, she was now imagining may have had a more devious purpose – a ride on the moors with his fellow thieves. At first, it had seemed impossible to her that he should be the highwayman, but she was beginning to suspect that there was no other explanation for his late-night sortie.

"Thank you, Bess. I have no reason to doubt that you will keep me informed, but what else do you know about it? Who do you suppose it could be?"

"Oh, Miss, I have heard stories, horrible stories about him. The highwayman," Bess said as she lowered her voice. "He is the master of a gang of thieves, as cruel and mean as they come. But it's the master who is the villain. He has even been called a murderer. I've heard that he is a cutthroat, and that he would run you through with his sword just for looking him in the eye." Bess glanced at her with one wide eye to put an emphasis on her sentence.

Catherine thought about her own experience with the highway-man and the duke. There was a remarkable similarity between the encounters. They were remarkable, not only for the similarity of their actions but also for something else ... something she could not quite recall as she pressed her maid for more information,

"What does he look like? Has anyone seen him without his mask?"

"Well, I have heard many a person declare they know how he looks. I do not know for certain. But..." Bess paused as if she was telling a thrilling story, " ... I have heard it from people who say they know, that he has hair as black as night, as dark as coal, and that his eyes are the colour of the knife on his belt, and that he's as big as a bear. I heard tell that he has a voice that people say they can feel in their bones, and that it is like hearing the devil himself speak. As for the looks of his men – no one seems to talk much about them."

"His eyes are grey – is that what you mean?" asked Catherine.

"That's what I have heard, grey like a knife. They are as hard and sharp as the sword he uses to carry out his dark deeds – to run his victims through if they give him a reason to."

"What about the size of the man? You described him as big as a bear? You do know what a bear is? It is enormous."

"I've seen a bear at a fair, Miss. I know what one of those beasts look like and I stick by what I said to you. He's as big as a bear – that's what people say, that he's the tallest man you've *ever* seen. He can lift a grown man right off his feet."

Catherine thought of the duke. He was a tall man. He possessed broad shoulders and a muscular build. The duke's eyes were grey. He had thick, lustrous dark hair, and a voice that was commanding. It seemed like a ridiculous idea that a gentleman who was in possession of immense wealth, and who was the owner of a vast personal fortune and an enviable title, would risk hanging.

"Miss, I heard that he lives right here in Yorkshire, and that he's been outwitting the sheriff and the master himself, because he knows the moors better than anyone else. They say that he and his band of men move like haunts, appearing first in one place and then another ... with a speed no normal man could match. If you ask me, I think it's true what they say ... that he knows the roads and the lanes. I pray I'm not wrong, because if I am, it would mean that he's a servant of the devil ... that he's no man ... nor are the men who serve him." Bess shuddered as she finished her statement.

"Bess, you do not really think he is a servant of the devil?"

"I pray he is not, but he must be, if he's not a man! If he moves like they say he does ... *as swiftly as a ghost*. What else could he be? But Miss Catherine, you yourself must know something of him, you've seen him with your own eyes!"

"How long have these attacks been happening? Perhaps that will provide an answer to the mystery about him."

"I cannot say, Miss, but I seem to recall it hasn't been that long. There have always been lawless men about the moors ... but attacks by highwaymen haven't happened in these parts for a great many years."

Catherine finished her tea. Her mind was a whirl of strange thoughts. Not that she shared any of that with Bess. How could she tell the maid (or anyone else for that matter) that she suspected the Duke of Rotherham of being the highwayman? A common criminal who attacked coaches and travellers whenever the mood struck him, or perhaps when he fancied a bit of adventure to pass the time, in a vile pursuit? Catherine feared that she may reveal too much if she spoke of him. Her own enthusiasm for the mystery of the highwayman's identity must remain concealed, if she was to remain unsentimental about any conversation she may have about His Grace.

Consumed by her new interest in discovering the purpose of the duke's secret errand, she soon forgot much else. The subject of the highwayman was far too fascinating, especially when she suspected it might be the duke. She laughed to herself, to think she might confront the man who seemed to dislike her so much, with this vital piece of information.

How delightful would it be to see him brought to justice? If, in fact, he *was* the highwayman (for what reason, she still could not comprehend), she would enjoy being the one person who knew the truth, and the one person who could – if she chose to – seal his fate.

Chapter 10

Catherine's exhilaration in believing that she may be the only person who knew the truth about the identity of the highwaymen's leader, was temporarily interrupted by an undignified meeting with her uncle. Before Catherine had even left her bedroom, a footman relayed the message that her uncle had asked to see her. It was awful timing. She felt hungry and wanted another cup of tea. As she left her room to see her uncle, Catherine made her way along the landing – the same place where she had nearly fallen the previous evening. She paused for a moment to reflect on her chance encounter with the duke, and about how demanding and threatening he had been towards her. How dare he accuse her of following him! Only a villain, a criminal, or someone with a secret, would be afraid of being followed.

Her uncle was as intimidating as ever. *If she had been fortified by sleep and her mother's presence,* she thought to herself, *she may have been able to endure her uncle's stern face and sharp criticism with grace rather than indignation and impotent anger.* Without her mother at her side, she was forced to bear the brunt of her uncle's disapproval alone, with no one to shield or defend her – not that she suspected her mother would do either. Instead Catherine sat in her uncle's study, wishing to be anywhere else other than across from a man she did not trust.

"I am disappointed ... profoundly disappointed in you. I have given you every opportunity to make the most of the company ... and you have failed to do so," the Viscount of Wharton said in a tone that implied that he was seething.

"Sir, I do not understand your disappointment," she replied.

"Have you? I sincerely doubt that. I have seen no fruit come from your paltry efforts."

Although intimidated by him and nervous in his presence, Catherine was also exhausted. Especially now, when she was not entirely herself, nor able to hold her temper under control. It seemed as if even her bones ached. She could feel her cheeks burning red with indignation.

"I have disappointed you? What would you have me do? I have done all that I could to secure the attention of the Duke of Rotherham! But if you are not pleased with my efforts, perhaps I should leave. I can do so immediately!"

He slammed his fist down on his desk, causing her to jump, as he spat out the next words, "I brought you here to my house out of kind and honest interest, to see that your future is secure, and *this* is how you repay my generosity?"

Catherine was in dangerous waters – she knew that. Was it her fatigue – the result of several sleepless nights – or frustration, or both, that caused her to forget her upbringing as she addressed her uncle? She had been taught from an early age to regard her father, and any gentleman, with the deference that their sex and their rank deserved. Her uncle deserved respect. If she behaved as she knew she ought, she should have been weeping at the mere thought that she had disappointed him. However, Catherine was not that woman, at least not this morning. Even at the risk of being exiled from Brigham Park, and of facing a future without the viscount's aid for her mother, she would not hold her tongue. She stood her ground in a way that her uncle or anyone else would consider impudent, at the very best. Why was she being forced to pay attention to a reprehensible nobleman such as the duke, when she would have a far easier time pursuing a pleasant but unassuming fellow such as the Earl of Burwickshire, who despite his lack of physical attributes, was an amiable sort of man?

Brushing aside her anger, she replied in a trembling voice, but one that would not be silenced, "If I understood the reason behind your generosity, and the cause of your insistence that I speak to no one but His Grace, perhaps I might be able to do as you say. Why is it necessary that I humiliate myself by pursuing a gentleman who cares not one whit for me? Would I not be better served by turning my attention to another gentleman? I have observed that there are other unmarried men in the party, who may not share His Grace's poor opinion of me."

"Other gentlemen?" He snorted, his disgust evident. "There is not one other gentleman in the party who is nearly as wealthy and as well-connected as the duke. I expected a woman in your position to understand what was being offered to her."

The seemingly benevolent benefactor her uncle had portrayed upon her arrival had disappeared. All that was left was this furious man who sat across from her. He had pounded his fist on his desk, scowled at her and spoken to her as if she was not of his own family. Catherine examined what he had said. She came to the conclusion that she was no closer to understanding his motives than before he had demanded that she join him in the study. Just as she opened her mouth to say so, he continued without waiting for her to respond to his previous statement.

"You and I are alone. I will not waste time by speaking with niceties or pleasantries. Your mother – I dare say, your entire family – is in a state of financial ruin. Your mother has confided the extent of her circumstances to me. You may be aware, or perhaps you are far too frivolous to comprehend – your family may yet be saved. But it will depend on your marriage. If you are matched with the right sort of gentleman, you may save your family from poverty and embarrassment. If you are foolish, you will be the sole reason your family becomes destitute."

Catherine's mouth dropped open in shock. Then, she slowly closed it again and stared at her uncle with a growing sense of revulsion. When she finally found her voice, she replied, "You are accusing me of being frivolous, and of ignoring my duty to my family? I am well aware that marriage to a gentleman of wealth and connection may save my family, but I will not shoulder a burden that I had no part in creating, if it comes at this high a price."

"You ungrateful girl! Do you not care to save your family, or do you think solely of yourself?"

"I am not ungrateful. I will not permit you to say that I do not care about my family when I would do all that is in my power to save us from ruin."

"I wonder," the viscount replied, and his lips curled into a thin frown, "if you *are* doing all that you can. I would be willing to arrange a generous allowance for your mother, if I knew that you were determined to ensnare the duke. As pitiable as your circumstances have become, surely even you must be aware that he is the only gentleman capable of salvaging your family's estate."

"What of the earl, or a viscount? What of someone who was not titled a duke?"

"You would be wise to avoid any conversation with the men who possess those titles, and who are guests in my house. Your obstinacy is trying. Do not test me on this, or your mother and your family will starve, before I send a penny for your bread."

Her uncle was incredibly stern. He moved quickly and demonstrated that he was just as terrifying as Catherine recalled. He rose quickly from his desk, and stood towering over her as he demanded, "For you, my dear Catherine – my niece – there is no one else at this house except Rotherham. Your laziness and insistence on openly disobeying me, will no longer be tolerated. Find some way to win the duke's hand, or your family will suffer for it. Now go. Leave my study. I have no wish to speak to you until you have succeeded in your efforts. If you fail to do as I have asked, I think you and I understand each other – the consequences for your family will be severe."

Catherine was glad that her uncle had asked her to leave his study. She had no desire to remain in his presence, especially after he had used his height and his demeanour to try to scare her. The revulsion she was beginning to feel for him, had turned to disgust.

But what could be done? He was the wealthiest relative her family had. If he did not help them, nobody else would. She really had no choice but to comply with his demands. Worse, Catherine doubted she had the slightest chance of succeeding. She had no other option but to remain at Brigham Park, in the clutches of her vile uncle.

The duke, her uncle, and her future were all part of a perplexing problem – one she grappled with as she left her uncle's study. Ordinarily, she would have been shaken and trembling from fear and despair after an interview as discouraging as the one she just endured. For some unknown reason, however, she rather felt bold and vexed by the interruption to her planned morning schedule.

She was keen to eat breakfast, even though her head was filled with her uncle's impossible demands and her family's impending ruin. She needed to enjoy a simple meal before she returned to coping with the myriad of problems that she faced.

She walked through the great hall, heading towards the breakfast room to partake of that meal. As she approached the room, she saw a tall, fashionably dressed man leaning casually against the banister of the main staircase. She slowed her pace. She noticed that the gentleman was dashing in a debonair, careless sort of way. Catherine doubted that the gentleman had seen her, as he was addressing a woman who was as stunning and gaze-riveting in her countenance as he was. Both of them were busy overseeing the footmen, who were bringing in a large pile of trunks. They both had the same shade of light hair, the same lithe frames, and appeared to be nearly the same age. Catherine assumed them to be brother and sister, but she did not want to pry into their private conversation and so she attempted to go around them. Moving as unobtrusively as she could, Catherine tried to walk around the gentleman and his fashionable companion, attempting to slip by unnoticed. But as soon as she stepped one way, the handsome man moved in the same direction.

They collided.

"Oh, I did not see you there. Do excuse my clumsiness! Are you hurt?" the gentleman asked Catherine. "Did I injure you?"

Catherine smiled. "The fault was entirely my own. I should have looked where I was going."

"Oh, but you did. I saw you!" the glamorous woman said as she stepped towards Catherine. "My brother was not paying the slightest attention to anything but our trunks," she declared loudly. "We have not been properly introduced ... but, I see no reason not to do this ourselves, since we are both staying here at Brigham Park. I am Margaret Churchill. This ill-behaved brute is my brother, Alcott." Her questioning gaze was Catherine's cue to follow with her own introduction.

"I am Miss Catherine Conolly." Catherine introduced herself but decided not to mention her connection to the Keelings – not after her interview with her uncle had ended so terribly. Upon closer inspection, Miss Margaret Churchill was not only elegant in a conventional manner, but she was a beauty! Her light hair was curled around her brow, while the remainder of her light-coloured locks were hidden under a green bonnet that matched her fur-trimmed pelisse and her carriage dress. An equally sumptuous fur-lined muff was carelessly thrown onto a table in the hall, with a matching reticule lying haphazardly on top of it. Her gloves were taupe, and her cheeks were as rosy as a perfectly ripe apple. Speaking to her, Catherine immediately noticed her confident air, evident in her twinkling dark eyes and radiant, engaging smile.

"Run along, sister dear, you have a mountain of trunks that require your attention. Leave the introductions to me," Mr Churchill said with a broad grin spread across his handsome face.

"Alcott, do be sure to greet Denton Keeling for me, and his dear father," Margaret said to her brother before her gaze fell on Catherine once again. "It was a pleasure to make your acquaintance. Do not let my brother's audacity fool you – he really *is* quite sweet."

Catherine smiled in reply. She did not know who the brother and sister pair were, but obviously they knew the Keelings quite well. "You speak of the viscount and his son as though they were family."

"I have not given the matter any consideration," Mr Churchill replied casually. "In answer to your inquiry, we are well aquainted with them, but that is to be expected. Our house is not far from here. We have lived close to Brigham Park for generations. In my youth, I spent just as much time at this house as I did at my own." Mr Churchill nodded to Catherine in a friendly manner. "But I am speaking to you without considering what you were doing, or where you were going before we met, aren't I? I have a habit of speaking freely to any woman I find as handsome as you, Miss...? I am sorry..."

"Conolly."

"Miss Conolly, you were walking through the hall when I stumbled into you. Where were you going?"

"Breakfast," she answered with a smile, just as she felt her stomach rumble.

"Breakfast at this late hour? I hope you have not missed it ... or myself for that matter. I am famished! But do not worry, if we have missed breakfast, it should not be any trouble to receive breakfast whenever we demand it."

Mr Churchill spoke with the same confidence that his sister exuded. Catherine's initial reaction to him, apart from the obvious appreciation for his handsome features, was that he seemed somewhat arrogant. He was also flirting with her outrageously. Catherine was not naïve about the ways of gentlemen: the way he smiled, his lingering glances, and the penetrating gaze of his gleaming eyes as he looked at her. She knew how some men (besides the duke, that was) usually acted in her presence – adoration, charm, and compliments. Mr Churchill clearly demonstrated he had noticed her by escorting her to the breakfast room, and he then remained with her as she drank her tea and dined.

Chapter 11

Alcott Churchill proved to be a popular gentleman in the drawing room. Women naturally flocked to him. His personality was warm, his laugh cheerful, and he was remarked as being amongst the most handsome men at the party. By the evening, and before dinner was served, Catherine discovered that not only was Mr Churchill a popular man, but he was also well received by her cousin and her uncle. He also chose to remain at her side (or near her) for the afternoon and into the night – or so it would appear.

In a similar fashion, his sister was at the side of the Duke of Rotherham from the moment she first graced the drawing room with her radiant presence.

However, even though the pair was undeniably charming, mastering all forms of parlour games and cards since their arrival, Catherine found the task of impressing the duke far more formidable than it had been earlier. Mr Churchill proved to be an attentive new acquaintance and kept her occupied. Lady Frederica also seemed drawn to Mr Churchill, and so she was compelled to remain near Catherine because of him. Each time Catherine attempted an exit, Mr Churchill proposed a compelling amusement that meant Catherine had to remain in his company.

Rotherham, who was often to be found on the opposite side of the drawing room to Catherine, seemed to be always engaged in a conversation with Miss Churchill and several other ladies. To Catherine's despair, it was Miss Churchill's lilting laughter that was carried across the room. It was she, who was able to garner the duke's attention, whereas Catherine was unable to find a polite way to escape from the lady's brother. True, she did find Mr Churchill a fascinating man - charming, and witty as well, but there was something in his manner that was a little too familiar. Something in his behaviour, or his speech, that she found slightly unsettling.

If Catherine had been anywhere but Brigham Park, and taxed with the task of enchanting a duke into marriage, she may have had more time to consider what it was that Mr Churchill desired from her. Yet, it seemed that her mind was consumed with other concerns instead. Her major worry was the new secret she harboured regarding the identity of the highwayman. If she could only manage to slip into the duke's presence, charm him, and learn more about him, perhaps she could discover the truth about the man she believed was capable of horrendous crimes and hard cruelty. At the same time, she would satisfy her uncle's wishes.

Vowing to find some way to separate herself from Mr Churchill politely at dinner, Catherine was slightly shocked by the seating arrangements in the dining room. Mr Churchill and his sister were placed closer to Catherine than she would have anticipated, considering their connection to her uncle. From their placement at dinner, she ascertained that if either of them had a title, their rank had to be nearly equal to her own, although their fashionable clothes spoke of great wealth.

Their lowly seating at the dinner table was not the only surprise. For a second time, the duke did not appear at dinner. Curiosity surged through Catherine as she thought of what his strange behaviour could mean. Where had he gone at such a late hour again? Was he concerned with another robbery? Why would he miss dinner for a second time so conspicuously? Oddly, she seemed to be the only person who observed his absence. The dinner table conversation did not even remark on the missing duke. Conversely, it did include several attempts from Mr Churchill to engage Catherine in conversation. It appeared that he was fixated on her – and her alone.

After dinner, Catherine's mother cornered her in the drawing room. The older woman appeared quite distraught. When she was close enough to her daughter, she dug her fingers into Catherine's arm and pulled her into a dim corner before Mr Churchill and the other gentlemen made their appearance.

"Catherine," she whispered, as she drew her daughter away from the other guests, "what are you doing?"

"Mother?" Catherine asked, twisting her arm from her mother's pincer-like grasp.

"I am not going to permit you to ruin your chance, child! Your only chance! What are you thinking? You are not a princess. Rich men will not be flocking to your door to propose."

"I know, Mother," Catherine replied, rubbing her arm, as she adjusted her long glove to hide the emerging red marks of her mother's fingers.

"Then do as your uncle and I wish. You must find a way to gain the trust and interest of the duke. Please do not refuse my brother's help."

"Mother, your brother threatened to let us starve. Do you honestly believe me to be capable of callously ignoring our plight?"

"Yes, I do. I do believe it. I have seen it all day! You shamelessly flirt with a man who will do nothing to help your family. I have not the slightest doubt that you will find your way to his side this evening."

"Are you talking about the Earl of Burwickshire or about–?"

"No, do not be impertinent. You know of whom I speak. Mr Churchill of course! You have become inseparable from him. Your uncle is furious and so am I. If you do not cease to pay attention to this person, and start doing your duty to your family, I may have sufficient cause to disown you."

"You would disown me? Do you know what you are threatening?" Catherine gasped in shock.

"I do, and I mean what I say. Your disregard for your uncle's counsel has led me to this painful decision. Once vexed, your uncle will be unwilling to help our family. If you remain unwed, there can be no assistance from this direction, either. Our fate ... my future ... your family ... are relying on you, and yet you spend your time dallying with a man of little consequence."

Catherine was hurt by her mother's threat. She was also angered. "You would hold me to blame when I am unable to escape the attentions of Mr Churchill? He has his eye set on me and I have no idea why! If only you and my uncle would listen to me! The duke does *not* want to speak to me. He is distant towards me. He actively removes himself from my company when I am near. I believe him to be concerned with many things, the least of which is that he already harbours an affection for someone else. I simply cannot surmount these obstacles to gain what you and my uncle would have me achieve. Are you so blinded by the promises of your brother, that you do not see the frustration of your daughter?"

"Catherine," her mother hissed in a low tone, smiling at nearby guests who had begun entering the room, as though she and Catherine were engaged in a typical conversation between mother and daughter. "We did not come to Brigham Park so you could marry a man who has no, *or* a lower title, and who has no connections and not a trace of wealth. We came here to appeal to your uncle's generosity and loyalty, and consequently, to find you a husband. Are you so obstinate and wicked that you refuse your uncle's efforts to see you are made a bride, and your family is saved from ruin?"

"Mother, I am not stubborn. I am exhausted by the task that neither of you will concede is a failure. Can you not understand? There is nothing to be done to win the duke. Nothing at all. Please stop listening to your brother. He poisons you against me by dangling the promise of a living over you."

"I am prepared to do what I must to see the family through. I suggest you do the same," Lady Conolly stated, and she walked away from her daughter. Catherine stood silently, trembling in the dimly lit corner of the drawing room.

"Disowned, unmarried, and unloved," Catherine whispered to herself. Those were the consequences of ignoring her uncle's demands.

As she stood in shock at her own mother's betrayal, speculating that it was due not to a lack of maternal feeling, but rather inspired entirely by fear of an uncertain future and financial ruin, Catherine's interest in the duke was renewed. Not because of matrimony – that was a cause that was as lost as her own hope of a happily contented future. Her interest was borne of an entirely different intent.

With her own future looking so dark and – in her eyes, hopeless – she felt driven to discern his true identity. She did not act out of any excitement that may be gained from seeking the truth. Nor did she suspect him to be a criminal, solely because that course of action was a better alternative than being chastised by her uncle. If the duke was proven to be the highwayman and arrested, his name and reputation would be besmirched, and she could not be expected to marry such a man.

But her interest in the duke was fuelled by more than self-preservation. She wished to end this man's reign of fear and terror, and to reveal to the world that this man – this *gentleman* who commanded respect with his grand title and wealth – was no better than a thief! This was what drove her to decide that her previously slight interest in the duke's nocturnal habits must be forged into something far stronger. Her interest in the Duke of Rotherham was now a quest for the truth.

And it was up to Catherine to expose His Grace for the man he truly was – a criminal.

Chapter 12

The duke did not return to play cards, even though the drawing room was lively that night. Catherine hid the pain she had felt at her mother's cruel words behind her fascination at Lady Frederica's attempts to engage Mr Churchill, who was, himself, flirting shamelessly with Catherine. Her mother and uncle glared at her from time to time, despite the absence of Rotherham. As the hour grew late, Catherine made the customary excuses to retire, after the older women had gone up, but before the younger members of the party.

She wished to find a suitable place to conceal herself until later that night. Catherine wanted to be able to observe the duke, should he return from another night-time errand. This time, she would not be found, she decided. She needed to make sure that he would not have another opportunity to confront her in the darkness.

Catherine escaped the room while Mr Churchill was occupied by a rousing game of cards (which he happened to be winning against the Earl of Burwickshire). As she left the drawing room, she knew time was of the essence. She needed to find a place to hide where she could observe, but where she would not be seen. There was the small sitting room and there was the library. Unfortunately, neither room offered a view of the staircase, but if she was correct about the duke, he undoubtedly would not be back from his dreadful escapades until the very late hours. This made the sitting room the more suitable hiding place. Catherine quickly slipped into the dark, cold room, which was not lit by fire or candle. Moonlight filtered in through the windows as she closed the door, leaving the tiniest crack to observe anyone who may pass by.

The cold stone walls behind the garden-inspired tapestries were as ice to the touch. Without the warmth of a fire, Catherine felt a chill that caused her to question her choice of such a desperate quest. Should she go up to her room and rest for an hour or two in the warmth of her fireplace and under the covers before returning to wait for the duke? No. She decided she could not risk being seen by anyone as she exited her hiding spot and walked to her room. It was far better if it was assumed that she was safely tucked into her bed, than to be found wandering the dark corridors at a late hour.

The night crept slowly by as she stood shivering in the cold room. In the dark, she had nothing to distract her from the confusion of her own thoughts. Rotherham's earlier response on the landing had been anger – and something else. How dreadfully he had treated her! Had he sincerely thought she would be foolish enough to reveal his (and her own) late night excursion? If he desired his odd late-night riding habits to remain a secret, perhaps he should not have been strolling through the great hall so boldly, without a care of being seen by anyone. What was it about her that vexed him so completely that he seemed to go through great pains to avoid her at all other times?

She closed the door silently, after she heard the footfalls of the last guests on the stone pavers. In chattering groups, they left the drawing room, destined for their bedrooms. Their laughter and conversation wafted away from her, becoming distant. Now, the room was entirely dark, and she was chilled. What would she do if she discovered the duke returning from the moors? Confront him? She had not decided on her course of action, but in the back of her mind, she was beginning to grow concerned that he may simply be spending a quiet evening in his chamber.

Catherine dismissed the thought from her mind as quickly as it had come. She did not wish to think that her suffering was for nothing. She did not believe he was in his room. Despite her misgivings about him and her certainty that he was wicked, she was consumed by a curiosity about him that she had to satisfy. What a conflicted tangle of feelings and emotions she had within her breast! How was he able to mesmerise her so, yet also cause her to wish him brought swiftly to justice?

His obvious contempt for her pained her more than she cared to admit. So far, she had not thought about him in endearing terms. In fact, in all her years, she had never known anyone as overbearing and distant as he. His disdain, which was never rude, but which was colder than the dark moors, or indeed the wall she currently leaned upon, was a source of fascination to her. He repelled her and yet drew her in. How she wished she had the power to avoid him.

Catherine's thoughts were interrupted by the sound of steps approaching the sitting room. She saw her cousin, Denton, and the viscount. Once more, she was made aware of her odd behaviour, lurking about in a cold, unlit room and, suddenly, she was afraid she would be caught. That would lead to questions she had no wish to answer, especially if she were interrogated by her uncle or her cousin. Steeling herself for an inevitable discovery, she closed her eyes and shrank back from the door. To her relief, they passed by the sitting room. She sighed and felt ridiculous. The sounds of merrymaking and laughter had dissipated. So, she presumed that the last two members of the party, who were downstairs, were her uncle and cousin. She could hear that they had turned off the hallway and had entered the study. To her astonishment, the door to the study was left open. They either had no desire to conceal their conversation, or they were certain they were the last awake at the late hour. Their voices were muffled, but when Catherine widened the narrow crack of the door carefully and listened intently, she heard her name.

Straining to hear the remainder of their conversation, she opened the door as far as she dared but could not discern another word – the conversation was still muffled. Dare she sneak out of the sitting room? What if a footman found her listening to the viscount's private discussion? Or, what if the duke returned from his awful late-night ride on the roads?

Catherine was willing to accept the consequences in order to hear why she was being discussed. She recalled how her cousin had denied any knowledge of her uncle's motives. She snuck out of the sitting room and crept past the library towards the study. A table and chair that were placed against the stone wall afforded her some protection from being seen. She crouched down, leaning as close as she dared to the door that hung ajar. Luckily, the house was quiet, and their voices carried in the cold night air.

It seemed her uncle was livid and was in the middle of revealing his fury to his son.

"That girl is proving to be useless," said the viscount. "I have wasted my time in inviting her. If I had known she was so opinionated, I would never have wasted my effort."

"Father, she is your niece. I have never questioned you, but what has she done to earn your disapproval? I have witnessed nothing that leads me to believe that she does not conduct herself as a proper young woman of her rank."

"A proper young woman? What I require is a woman who is willing to do what she *must*, to secure the hand of a young man. How difficult can such a task be? She is beautiful – as beautiful as the reports I received from her first season in London. With her pleasing countenance and her connection to me, the duke should have proposed the first night he saw her!"

"I have observed them together ... Rotherham is not swayed by her beauty."

"That is a failing that I attribute to her. A woman as comely as she is, and who wishes to better her position through an advantageous marriage, would not allow a man such as Rotherham to slip through her hands so easily."

Catherine heard the voice of her cousin answering, his confusion as evident as her own. "But why him? Why are you angered regarding the trivial matter of your niece's prospects? She is an intelligent young woman who does not have much fortune to offer, but she *does* have ambition. She would do well in a match to any number of gentlemen. I would not consider a match with a suitable gentleman other than the duke to be regrettable."

"Regrettable," the viscount said. His disgust was audible, even from her hiding place. "Denton, I am astounded that you are not capable of understanding what is at stake if your lovely cousin does not do her duty to me *and* to you. This estate, this house, and everything that has been in the Keeling family for countless generations are in jeopardy."

"I knew we were having difficulties ... but I did not know we ... risked losing Brigham Park. Why, Father? Is there nothing to be done?"

"Calm down. Now you understand the pain of enduring my sister. Her marriage is the reason that she now finds herself impoverished, yet she asks me for an allowance. She imagines her children should be supported by me, or hopes that, because she presumes upon my brotherly affection for her. I have no interest in providing an allowance to her or any of her brood, all of whom are barely Keelings, in my opinion. Why would I waste those funds when we need them ourselves at this time? I may be inclined to offer my sister a gift, but I will *not* do so without an effort being made from their side – and that effort is being obstinately refused by Catherine. The girl simply snubs the duke, and it is a match that would save her own wretched family from starvation on the streets, as well as Brigham Park."

"What? The Duke of Rotherham?"

"What indeed? Are you naïve, Denton? Rotherham, how I loathe saying that, is our rival in court and in county. He wants this estate, to laud his victory over our family."

Catherine covered her mouth with her hand to keep from gasping out loud.

"If we lose it, it will be because he has acquired it," the viscount continued. "I do not relish being turned out of my home by the man whose father I hated and whose grandfather I sincerely despised. Do you not understand, Denton, the necessity for my niece to win his hand?"

"I fail to understand what my cousin can possibly do to save our estate," Denton replied. "She has no wealth of her own, and His Grace is adamantly opposed to her."

"Denton," he sighed, "you fail to see my plan because of your sentiment for her. Your temperament is far too compassionate. Do you not understand that should Rotherham marry her, he would then find it impossible to seek our ruin? He would be connected to our family by marriage, an alliance he could not ignore, either in court or here in Yorkshire.

"But that niece of mine does not obey me. How I wish I had never seen or invited her here. If I was endowed with a more suitable niece, or indeed any other relation to offer him, I would not hesitate, but as it stands, she is the only woman I have to offer. Her beauty should recommend her, but it has not. Her personality is both far too independent ... and dull."

"That is your interest in your niece? Do you not care for her happiness or whether she might secure a marriage to a count or a baron? Is that why she must marry the duke?"

Catherine trembled with indignation as she listened to her uncle's reply. "She is bait, Denton, and nothing more. I have no care for the girl or my sister, but I must use what resources I have. Rotherham has stated that he intends to purchase Brigham Park, and he will have it if we do nothing – and I do not intend to do nothing. I do not have any natural desire to claim her as my niece, but yet I am forced to do so. She is essential to my plan. She must marry Rotherham. The future of Brigham Park depends on it."

A cascade of emotions flooded Catherine as she tried to make sense of all that her uncle had said to Denton. He had called her *bait*.

Her uncle despised his own sister and her family. He had simply been tolerating both of them for his own ends. Now that the reason for his invitation and his anger with her were revealed, Catherine was furious. She was tempted to march into the study and confront her uncle, but she could not – her mother was depending on him for an allowance or a gift, which would surely never come if she were to allow her emotions to overcome her good judgement. Those same emotions were building and churning at such a terrible rate, that she feared what she might do, and what may happen.

She wanted to yell at her uncle. She wanted to say what she felt but she could not. At the same time, she wanted to run away to escape from this place. She wanted to be away from the dreadful man and this house. The entire affair was far too much to be endured.

Carefully, or as carefully as she could manage, she left her place behind the table. She needed to be anywhere, anywhere but in that unbearable house, and think of what could be done. It was the only thing that made sense to her at that moment. As she rushed through the cold, dark house, she forgot about the duke and his night-time activities and her own physical discomfort in the cold night air. She wanted to be free of everything that plagued her: her family's dire financial circumstances, her uncle's cruelty, and the duke's indifference. She was tired of it all and she felt drained, alone, and terribly distressed.

Quietly hurrying through the gloomy hall of Brigham Park, she did not know where she was going, but she knew that she desperately needed some fresh air.

Chapter 13

Catherine found herself in the courtyard. She gasped as she tried to catch her breath in the frigid night air. She had run from the house, without care or concern for the outside, and now she was nearly doubled over from the effort. Her muscles, which had been seized by the hours of cold in the sitting room, were burning in agony. She stood still, trying to breathe, and inhaled the freezing-cold air into her lungs. Her heart was thumping so loudly that she was certain it would wake the entire house.

Now she understood her uncle's reason for forcing her to chase after the duke in a display that was not only humiliating, but which she was certain had appeared most pitiable. If only she could remove her uncle's words from her head! She knew the truth now, but what was to be done about it?

Slowly, Catherine found she could breathe again without her lungs feeling as if they were on fire. She turned her face upwards, gazing at the stars that filled the night sky. They were magnificent. There were so many of them, that the whole sky was glittering. There were no clouds that night, so there was nothing to obscure the beauty of the cosmos, whose permanent beauty brought a feeling of comfort to her own world, where her future was far from certain. Shivering, she folded her arms as she peered into the heavens. If only her life was as simple and easy as the lives of the other young women who were sleeping in their beds. What joy it would be to concern herself with such matters as finding a husband on her terms. Slowly Catherine began to feel better as she stood outside.

She knew she had to return to her room before she froze to death or caught a terrible chill. But that was a more troubling concern – how was she to return to her room without being seen? Where were her uncle and her cousin now? What time did the servants wake to begin their daily duties, especially the scullery maids who were tasked with building the fires in the rooms before the guests woke?

Despite the cruel circumstances of her life and her family's misfortune, which weighed heavily upon her, she returned to thinking about His Grace. Had the duke slipped back inside the house? Had she failed to see him? Oh, she hoped she had not missed the duke, but she consoled herself with the thought that if she had, she would continue her vigil the following night. If she could prove that he was the highwayman, her uncle would not lose Brigham Park to his rival, and she would be free from his plan. Settling on the plan that she should continue her quest to discover the duke's true identity, was far more agreeable than dwelling on her present troubles. As she turned to go back inside, she noticed someone or something in the darkness. There was a movement from the direction of the stables.

Exhilaration gripped her as she prayed that what she was seeing was a person and not an apparition, and that the person had not seen her blatantly standing in the night air observing the stars. Catherine quickly searched for some place that would offer her a scrap of shadow to conceal her presence and found a suitable hiding place in a narrow passageway. Its dark gaping entrance offered her a quick place to step out of sight.

She heard the unmistakable sound of footsteps on the stone pavers of the courtyard. The movement she had seen was one person approaching quickly. Hastily, she pressed her body against the freezing-cold stones of the walls. She prayed that she had not been seen, as she willed herself to hold her breath. Who was it? She heard the person walking across the courtyard, coming closer. Carefully, she peered in the direction of whomever was striding so confidently, their head up, despite the cold wind.

It was him. Catherine recognised the man she had been waiting for. His Grace, the villain, was walking across the courtyard, coming from the direction of the stables and approaching her. His features became clear as he drew closer. A single torch burned over his head, in a metal sconce on the wall beside a doorway. It illuminated his face and, she hoped, did not reveal her presence. She wanted to jump out to confront him, but she had no wish to replay yesterday's scene from the landing.

If he *were* the highwayman – and he must be – for what else could account for his odd nightly errands, it was dangerous (and admittedly, quite thrilling) that she alone knew his secret. A secret that she would soon reveal to the magistrate and her uncle, as soon as she discovered whether there had been an attack this same night. Oh, how exuberant she suddenly felt, but she knew she had to be careful. If he was coming back from a raid, he would undoubtedly be armed with a pistol, and she dared not let herself imagine what other terrible weapons he carried. Would he kill her, as he had threatened to do on the road? He could easily dispatch her without a witness, if he sought to protect his dreadful secret and to save himself from the hangman's rope.

Catherine tried to be brave. She reminded herself that if she could manage to prove the duke was a thief, then all her problems would disappear. It was an outrageous plan – an ambitious scheme. It was also slightly ridiculous to hope it would succeed, especially if she could not keep herself from being caught by her quarry. Bait indeed, she said to herself silently. If she was going to be used as bait, it was to be for her own ends and not her uncle's.

Willing herself to be silent, and not to even breathe, lest the sound of it reveal her presence, she stayed as motionless as a statue until the Duke of Rotherham had passed by, without hesitation or a glance in her direction. She heard the creaking of the ancient hinges of the large wooden door that led into the hall.

Then it was silent.

She was alone and she had witnessed the duke out at an ungodly hour. She had not been caught by him, and he had not witnessed her going against his demands that she not follow him. Feeling much better about her surveillance efforts, she waited for a few more minutes until she was certain that the duke must have gone upstairs to his room. Carefully, she slid out of the narrow passage and walked to the door. She opened it slowly, mindful of the creaky hinges. They stayed silent. She slipped through the smallest crack that she could manoeuvre between the heavy wooden door and its frame, nearly snagging her dress. Once she was inside, she had one task left: to sneak up to her room without being caught or seen by anyone.

She crept along silently, staring anxiously into the dimly lit hall, but she did not see anyone. There was no sign of the duke, her uncle or her cousin, or any servants. All she could see was the faint light of candles in a sconce on the wall, and the low light of the hearth fire in the hall. Other than that, there was no indication that she was not alone in the eerie darkness. She approached the stairs and the landing and studied the stairs as carefully as she could for any evidence that the duke had not gone up. She could not bear to be caught a second time! She feared whatever dreadful repercussions would befall her if she was discovered by the villain.

With every sense heightened, her focus was on reaching the stairs and climbing them without making a noise. Just as Catherine began to make her way towards them, she heard a sound behind her. It was a sound that was quick and unexpected in the darkness and she jumped in fright. She would have screamed, but a hand was clamped over her mouth. Then she was dragged into the darkness of the drawing room. She was not able to see the person's face, but she had a terrible feeling she knew the identity of her assailant.

It was undoubtedly the duke.

He had found her and now he intended to silence her forever.

Catherine tried to cry out, but she could not. The hand over her mouth was too strong. A thousand thoughts rushed through her head, and each one was worse than the one before. She struggled in vain as she felt a man's strong arms grasping around her, preventing her from running away. She writhed and kicked and attempted to get away, but she could not fight against her much-stronger attacker. Her heart pounded in fear.

In the dim light of the dying candle flame, her attacker revealed himself in a hushed tone of voice. "Miss Conolly, you slippery little vixen." A voice whispered into her ear. "You *are* slippery, retiring from the drawing room early to do whatever, and with whomever. What are you still doing out at so late an hour? Forgive me for being dramatic, but I could not resist surprising you as you crept back from your night-time encounter. Do not scream or you shall reveal yourself to someone other than myself."

The manner of the man's speaking, the teasing lilt in his voice, and the flirtation, was not what she expected. As she was released from her attacker's powerful grip, and the large hand that held her mouth closed was removed, she turned around quickly to see her attacker. She was astonished to see a grinning, cheerful-looking Mr Churchill.

"I can keep a secret," he whispered with a grin.

"Mr Churchill!" she exclaimed.

In a lightning-fast move, he pressed her against the wall, his hand clamped back over her mouth. "Shh! My dear, do be quiet. Whisper if you must. You have no wish to be discovered, do you? Not after you have been so delinquent in going to bed. You have obviously been missing from your bedchamber for several hours. Where could you have been? That is a question that others would find most interesting, don't you agree? I shall remove my hand but do take care not to make too much noise, the footmen will be about soon."

His face was close to hers, as he leaned down.

She could smell a slight hint of wine (or was it brandy?) on his breath. Slowly he removed his hand from her mouth once again, as Catherine attempted to make sense of what was happening. A minute ago, she had been sneaking through the great hall taking care not to be seen, while avoiding being caught by the duke. Now, she was in the drawing room, her back against the wall with Mr Churchill standing not a foot away, which seemed strange and frightening to her.

Slowly, he removed his hand from her mouth.

"What on earth are you thinking, Mr Churchill? Why have you forced me into the drawing room?" she blurted out in a hushed voice.

"My dear Miss Conolly," he whispered back, "my intentions were entirely humorous. I wished to have a bit of fun since you were sneaking about. I am glad I took it upon myself to amuse myself, or you may have been discovered. The footmen make their rounds from time to time. I thought there may be another servant coming down the hall. If I had allowed you to remain at the staircase, you may have been caught with me, alone, in the middle of the night. That would never do for your reputation. I have saved your good name. I admit my method was – perhaps – a touch dramatic, but what a jape!"

"If you saved me from discovery, I thank you, but you frightened me. You also gave me an awful shock by pulling me into the drawing room. I thought you were–" She stopped herself as she realised that she had almost said *His Grace*.

His smile had a leering quality. "Who did you think I was? Someone you were meeting, someone you wished to keep secret?"

Catherine looked at him in silence.

"Ah, Miss Conolly, do you have secrets? I think you do. No respectable woman would be roaming the house at such an hour, not unless she was meeting someone. Now that you and I are alone ... do tell me of your illicit escapades."

"Mr Churchill, I was not meeting anyone, and I have no secret," she replied, growing weary of his teasing.

"I do not mind if you have a secret, indeed, have as many as you like. I find women who are respectable, and who have few regrets to be dull company for a man such as myself – and with my tastes. You are not dull, are you, Miss Conolly?"

Catherine remained silent.

"Since we are alone, and are much better acquainted, I think I shall call you Catherine," he said as his grin became a smirk.

Catherine *was* aware that she was alone with Mr Churchill. In the drawing room, surrounded by a room full of people, she had found him less handsome than on the day she first saw him. His boldness, his sense of humour, and his refusal to leave her alone for even a moment, was tedious. In the drawing room late at night, with no one around, his presence was not only dreary, it was unnerving. He had already proved that he could overpower her. She shuddered to think of what more he was capable of, as he continued to signal disregard for decorum, by this presumed familiarity – a thought that was chilling. He wished to call her by her first name? That was a breach of protocol, and of all decorum. They were not well acquainted enough to warrant such familiarity. However, she realised that this was not the time to censure him, or to remind him of social custom.

"Mr Churchill, it is late. I must be going to bed," she said as she attempted to step closer to the door.

"I know the hour is late. I have been waiting for you for a long time. Did you know that? No, how could you have known that I have been searching for you? I was winning at cards when you slipped from my grasp. I was quite fortunate tonight. Since I was feeling lucky, I wanted to see if my fortune also extended to you, Catherine."

"You won? How delightful. You must be a lucky ... or a skilled card player. If you will excuse me, I must take my leave of you. The hour is indeed late, and I am in need of rest."

"It is late, but not too late for meeting someone. Is there a secret gentleman, Catherine? The man you have just left? Is that the reason that you require rest?"

"I have not been meeting anyone. You are mistaken," she replied, angered by his implications.

"*Have* I made a mistake? No. I do not think I am in error. I think I am right in my assumptions about you. You are the most beautiful woman I have ever laid eyes on, Catherine. But you are more than just an unusual beauty. I sense a passionate, unbridled nature hiding inside of you. I have seen how you speak, how you act, how you walk, and how you dance. You appear to be just like the rest of your kind, accomplished in the arts of music, cards, and tea. But what use do I have for that? I find those accomplishments to be utterly dull to a man of the highest standards such as myself. No, Miss Conolly ... Catherine ... I find a woman who has a similar appetite to my own to be far more interesting – especially a woman who does not mind taking a risk. You seem like that kind of woman. Tell me, whom did you meet tonight? Was it someone within my acquaintance – a gentleman from the party? Someone with a title and perhaps an inconvenient wife, or who is engaged to be married? No, that would be boring and predictable. Perhaps you were meeting someone your mother would find repugnant, such as a groomsman, or a valet?"

Catherine was shocked and insulted by Mr Churchill's scurrilous suggestions. How dare he imply the unthinkable – that she had a lover, or was meeting a married gentleman? Either suggestion required that she never speak to him again. She should not have to endure his presence or any more of his vile insinuations, but she was not where she should be – in her room. In her thirst to seek out the answer to the duke's mystery, she had exposed herself, not only to dreadful gossip, but something far worse. She had made herself vulnerable – something she had not imagined could happen, yet somehow it had. Now she was facing a man who had the effrontery to call her by her name and to suggest that she was capable of the worst sort of behaviour. Behaviour that was so shocking that she was appalled by the very mention of it!

"Come now, I enjoy a deliciously bawdy tale. Are you not going to tell me what I wish to know? You and I are friends now. You may rely on my discretion."

"I have nothing to tell you," she answered.

"You should reward me, Catherine. I am giving you my word that I will keep your secret."

"I have no secrets."

"We *all* have secrets. Shall I tell you a secret of mine – one I am sure that you will find fascinating?"

"I have no wish to hear it," she answered, feeling more and more certain that she was in a very precarious position.

"You will want to hear it. You will be glad that I have told you. It not only pertains to you, my dear Catherine, but to someone I believe you know quite well ... or rather you would like to. The Duke of Rotherham."

"The duke?" she asked.

"I have observed you when you were not watching me. How careless you are! You watch the Duke of Rotherham as a cat watches a mouse. I suspect that no one else would notice your interest in the man, of course, but I do! Nothing escapes my clever attentiveness. You should understand that it has been my duty to be observant of such things. My sister – you recall her – she is a beauty in her own right. She is ambitious. Margaret wants to become the Duchess of Rotherham. To ensure that her efforts are successful – and you must understand that I want her to succeed – I have used my exceptional knowledge of female behaviour to her advantage. Her marriage to a duke would improve my prospects, as well. Do you know how many eligible, wealthy young women would wish such a connection? I am certain you see how vital my role has been in this. I had to keep you occupied so that my sister had every chance to secure the duke's affections and her future as his wife."

Catherine no longer cared who heard her, or caught her as she hissed, "How dare you! How dare you speak to me as you have? You have insulted me on so many levels, and furthermore, you have confessed to thwarting me. I do not know what you wish to gain by revealing these things, but I care little to learn of it. Never speak to me again. I bid you goodnight, Sir." Furious, she turned to leave the drawing room.

He grabbed hold of her arm. His dark eyes gleamed. "Are you not forgetting something? I am a favoured guest of the viscount, and a neighbour, if you recall. Who are you? You are his poor relation. I am a gentleman who enjoys respect and admiration in this county. If I were to disclose that I found you ... shall I say, out and about this evening, *involved* in activities not suitable to be repeated in the presence of unmarried women – who do you think would be believed? We both know the answer. Your reputation would be ruined if I say one word."

She pulled her arm away from his tight grip and did not say anything in response as he continued. "There is no denying that you possess a natural grace and charm without artifice, and you have a fire that I can see in your eyes as you struggle against me. You are a spirited woman – intelligent and fascinating. I have no wish to ruin your reputation. I have a proposal I think you will find generous and acceptable, considering your current financial circumstances ... Ah, yes, I know all about you. Your family faces ruin, which is something I easily learned from your cousin. Your clothes are plain, but the impoverished nature of your attire does little to detract from your handsome features. That is the exact same reason that I had to distract you, while my sister claimed the duke for herself." He paused, and then Mr Churchill stared deeply into her eyes.

"Catherine, I am fascinated by your beauty. I no longer consider you my duty. I have other desires that involve you – desires that you will soon discover."

"I do not wish to hear your proposal. I find your actions and your words repugnant."

"My! How spirited you are, but you *will* accept my proposal. If you do not, the consequences would be too dreadful for you to bear. Financial ruin. Your reputation left in shambles. Then what will you do? You would not even find work as a governess or a maid."

"Mr Churchill." She attempted to interrupt him.

"As I was saying, my proposal is more than generous. I value women such as yourself – spirited and independent. I have no wish to force you into anything you may find objectionable. I am not a villain, but I do want to make you my mistress."

Catherine caught her breath in a wave of shock such as she had never experienced before.

"You wish me for your *mistress*? You insult me once again. I will not agree, Sir, to *anything* as vile as what you propose." She found the strength to say this, despite the tiny voice inside her head that suddenly cried out that she may not have a choice in the matter.

"Oh, but you *will* agree, dear. What choice do you have? I have caught you sneaking about the house in the middle of the night. Your reputation could be destroyed at my pleasure. I say, you will become my mistress or face ruin," he whispered as he leaned in close to her.

"I would rather face starvation than lose my honour and my dignity–" she said while the tiny voice became louder.

"What of your family?" He interrupted her. "Do you wish for them to starve so that you may retain your dignity? At what cost is honour, when you can accept my offer? Agree to my terms, or I shall see that your uncle evicts you from this house for your lascivious activities. You will wish you had said yes to me. Agree to my proposal and no one will have to know of our agreement. Your name will not be ruined – you have my word."

He was right. He could ruin her with a rumour, and she could do nothing about it. Catherine did not know what to do, she simply could not accept his proposal.

Not only did she find him repugnant, but she had no desire to be the mistress of *any* man. Her reputation, if it was not destroyed by gossip, would surely be ruined beyond all hope of redemption if it became known that she was any man's mistress. Catherine was nearly frantic with fear and panic and she closed her eyes, wishing for this whole terrible night to be over. She smelled the odour of alcohol, and she realised that Mr Churchill had leaned towards her, and that he was attempting to insult her further by kissing her. What a terrible thought! One far too dreadful to think about. She balled up her hands into fists as she prepared to strike the villainous Mr Churchill. The insult she was anticipating never came, and her eyes flew open as she heard the most unlikely of sounds – a man's voice coming from the direction of the doorway.

"Churchill, step away from Miss Conolly."

Chapter 14

His Grace the Duke of Rotherham was standing in front of her and Mr Churchill. He stated his demand a second time, "Churchill, I will not repeat myself. Step away from Miss Conolly."

"Your Grace ... this is a misunderstanding," Mr Churchill said with a smile.

"There is no misunderstanding, I believe. Miss Conolly, am I mistaken? Are you here of your own volition?" the duke asked her.

"Your Grace, I do not know what to say," Catherine replied, aware that with a single statement, Mr Churchill could leave her reputation in tatters (not that she would have much of a reputation left after being discovered alone with Mr Churchill in the drawing room by the duke of all people).

The duke addressed her again, "You do not have to answer my question. I overheard enough of the conversation to know that you are blameless in this matter."

"Blameless? This piece of soiled muslin?" Mr Churchill said. "Sir, you cannot think that I would be downstairs with a lady of a better reputation, do you? This woman lured me here into sin."

"She lured you?" The duke laughed at the man, as he drew near to him. "Mr Churchill, do not think me a fool."

The duke's manner rendered him imposing, as he towered over Mr Churchill. "I doubt that. I doubt every word you have said. I heard the threats you made to her and, unlike you, I know where she has been this evening. If you speak one word against her, one single word, I will see to it that you are ruined. I will use my influence to ensure that you are no longer received by any family in this county or in the realm. I promise you, when I am through with you, Mr Churchill, you will be fortunate to find work as a conscript in His Majesty's Navy."

"Your Grace! Would you take the word of this insignificant woman over me, a Churchill? You insult me. You threaten me with ruin when I have done no wrong. Nothing at all! What transpired between this woman and me is strictly a business transaction that women of her sort are accustomed to making, every day in the alleyways of London."

"How dare you!" Catherine exclaimed. She did not have to strike Mr Churchill, nor did she have to defend her own honour. To her complete and utter astonishment, the duke rose to his full height before the man who threatened her. In one fluid motion, he struck Mr Churchill so rapidly and so soundly that the man went flailing to the floor.

"Get up, you coward," the duke demanded in a tone of voice that implied that Mr Churchill had better not get up.

"Your Grace," Mr Churchill mouthed silently as he rubbed his jaw, "I ... I don't want to fight you."

"Stand so I may finish what you so rightly deserve."

"I ... I will not."

"Or you may yield – do you yield?" the duke said as he stood over Mr Churchill in a triumphant stance.

"I yield."

"Apologise to the lady or I shall not accept that you yield to me. Apologise at once, or you and I shall settle this matter of honour in the prescribed matter. Pistols or swords drawn will decide who is right, if you do not accept my terms. Are you prepared to accept them as readily as you threatened her with your scurrilous terms?"

"I accept them. I have no desire to meet you on the duelling field, not for a woman such as her," Mr Churchill spat.

"Get to your feet." The duke grabbed Mr Churchill's arm and pulled him roughly up from the floor. "You *will* beg her forgiveness until she is satisfied that you have grovelled enough for your insult to her. You will give *me* your word, as a gentleman, that you will never reveal what occurred in this room tonight. You will not discuss myself or Miss Conolly. You will not disclose that you found her about in the house late at night. You will not relate any of the scandalous stories that you have invented. From this night on, you will not speak of her to anyone. You will be polite to her, but you will no longer be bothersome. If I hear of a single incident that indicates that you have not complied with my terms, Mr Churchill, I will seek to settle this manner honourably. I should warn you: I am an excellent marksman."

Alcott Churchill was still rubbing his jaw as he looked at Catherine. The smirk was gone from his face. "Forgive me, Miss Conolly. My crimes against you are numerous and I renounce every one. I have insulted you gravely and I will never do so again – nor will I speak to you, or about you to anyone, for as long as I shall live."

"Is that acceptable? Do you wish to see him weep?" the duke asked her as he shoved the man to his knees. "Grovel, I say!"

As the frightened man knelt at her feet, Catherine replied, "That will not be necessary. Mr Churchill, please leave me alone and never speak to me again."

"Get out of here, you coward. Go before I dispatch you with my pistol," the duke said to the man, who was completely defeated.

Mr Churchill did as he was commanded. He rose to his feet and shuffled from the drawing room and up the stairs, thereafter he vanished from their sight.

Catherine stared at the duke. As if the entire evening had not been dreadful, now it was turning out to be astonishing enough to leave her confused for days. With the addition of the duke's saving her from a terrible fate at the hands of Mr Churchill, she was hoping she would never again see such a terrifying night.

"Miss Conolly, there is something I must ask of you. I will not inquire until you tell me you are recovered," he said as he led her carefully to a chair beside the dying embers in the hearth.

"You must be cold," he said as he removed his coat and placed the thick dark garment around her shoulders.

The fire was nearly dead. He stirred the embers until they glowed. "Shall I bring some more wood for the fire?"

"No, thank you. You have done enough. You have done more than enough. Sir, I should explain about Mr Churchill. What you witnessed was not how it appeared," she said as she pulled his coat around her.

His coat was black, like his clothes. He was dressed the part of the highwayman, but at that moment, she did not care about his dreadful secret. How could she allow herself to be concerned with his nocturnal activities after he had saved her from the evil designs of Mr Churchill?

"There is no need to explain yourself to me. I offer you my apologies that I overheard the conversation. I am afraid it could not be helped."

"There is no need to apologise. I dread to think what would have happened if you had not been listening. I do not know how I can ever repay your kindness."

"There is nothing to repay, but when you are ready, I do wish to ask you a question," he said as he drew near the fire.

With his coat around her shoulders, she began to feel warmer. She had spent so much time feeling cold that evening, that she had nearly forgotten what it felt like not to shiver. The whole night seemed as some kind of strange fevered dream. Her head was spinning, from exhaustion and from the events of the night. Each one was momentous in its own right, but put together, they were quite overwhelming.

"Miss Conolly, are you well? You are trembling."

"I am afraid the evening was rather much for me..."

"If you are unwell, I can see you safely upstairs. My question can wait. In all sincerity, it is not safe for you to be downstairs at this hour. The servants will be stirring soon, and the scullery maids will be about their duties. I have no wish to be the reason your reputation is ruined."

"I am well, Sir. I am merely in awe that you have saved me. I should be glad to answer any question you care to ask me," she replied.

"I do not wish to censure you, Miss Conolly. You are a woman who is capable of making her own decisions, regardless of the lack of foresight or judgement involved in that endeavour. I believe you understand my meaning."

"I do, Sir. I have not used the best judgement tonight."

"No, you have not ... which leaves me to my query. Why are you following me?"

Catherine was surprised to hear his question. Then she decided to confess the truth. "I am not sure if I should reveal my true reason for following you."

"I know that you could tell me some base falsehood. However, I do not have any cause to doubt you," he said. "I will believe you because I know your character and because of my faith in your good name."

"My good name, which almost came to an end this very night ... were it not for you," she said as she looked at him.

Strangely, he was not acting like a villain this evening. He had returned to the house from some strange and mysterious errand – that was true. He had no reason to defend her honour, no reason at all, and for that, she was grateful. Would a villain risk his own life to save a woman he did not care for? No, that was impossible.

After a few minutes of silence, she had gathered her thoughts. "I may be a fool for telling you the purpose of my surveillance. I may

—

regret it, but your actions tonight were honourable, which is contrary to what I thought of you. If I had been correct in my presumption of where I believed you to be, then you would have done nothing to rescue me. I know that I sound ridiculous, but I fear that I will not seem as pitiable as I do when I reveal the reason for my behaviour, Sir."

"I await your explanation," he said. "I am curious as to what could have led you into a surveillance of my private activities."

"My explanation is not a lengthy one. I shall say it quickly or I shall lose my nerve. I thought you might be the highwayman."

"The highwayman? I thought those thieves travelled in packs, like wolves," he replied.

"I suspected that you were their leader, and that you led the gang that attacked my mother and myself on the road, the night we journeyed to Brigham Park."

He stared at her. His expression was as unreadable as ever. Then he spoke. "I have no wish to insult you, but you are mistaken. I am not the highwayman."

"No, I know now that you are not," she said. "A highwayman would not have struck Mr Churchill for me, a woman without fortune."

"You are more fortunate than you realise. I was waiting for you on the landing. I knew you were outside in the courtyard. You may not have been aware, but I saw you as you gazed at the night sky. I made no sound because I did not wish to disturb you. You seemed to be entranced by the dazzling display of the heavens. I did not suspect you were following me until you ran and hid from me, and then crept inside the house behind me. At the time, I *was* angry that you would spy on me, again, after I had asked you to cease. It was at that moment that I observed Mr Churchill and yourself. I would have confronted him earlier, but when I first arrived at the drawing room door, I wrongly assumed you and he were ... shall I say ... well acquainted. I had already observed that he seemed to be attentive to you in the drawing room. It was not until I heard your rebuttal of him, that I knew something was terribly wrong."

"I am embarrassed that I ever thought you could be a lowly thief on the road," Catherine said. "How foolish you must believe me to be."

"Foolish? Not quite. In truth, I have given you no reason not to presume that I was the highwayman. My habits are unusual. I prefer to dress in dark clothes. I wear the same sombre colour I have heard that highwaymen favour."

"Yet it seems perfectly absurd now that I think about the matter. What reason could you possibly have to risk the hangman's rope for a few hundred pounds or someone's jewels? I cannot think of a motive, nor can I reconcile your actions tonight with those of a common thief."

"I would not say it was perfectly absurd. Perhaps you read too many novels?" he asked, and for the first time, Catherine saw his lips form into a friendly smile.

"Sir, if I may... perhaps you should not be sneaking around keeping late hours?"

"I will be careful in the future ... not to incite the imaginations of young women." He laughed.

When he laughed, she found his entire demeanour had changed. He was no longer a cold and distant aristocrat who barely noticed her. He was a man - a dashing man who had offered to duel the villainous Mr Churchill in order to defend her honour. How silly she had been! His laugh, even in its hushed tone, was contagious, and she began to laugh at her own folly.

Finally, he said, "We should take care. I fear we have been far too exuberant in our amusement."

"If I lose my reputation over laughing, then so be it. I have not laughed in days," she said, but did not disclose the reason for her unhappiness, as she tried to dismiss all thoughts of her uncle and his scheming.

"I was prepared to defend a lady's honour and her reputation with my pistol, if I had to. I have no wish that my actions should be in vain."

"I also hope that your actions are not in vain," she whispered. "Please forgive me for being as foolish as to accuse you of being a common thief."

"You are forgiven. In fact, you have astonished me with your unusual idea, Miss Conolly."

"Astonished or shocked?" she asked.

"Both," he confirmed. "Now, I must see you safely upstairs. But before we leave tonight, I will have your word – can you give me that?" he asked, the smile gone from his face.

"Sir, I owe you a great debt."

"Give me your word. Promise me that you will cease following me. I ask you that, not for selfish reasons, but because you risk more than your honour. It is not safe for a woman to walk around a large house at night without a chaperone. There are dangers, Miss Conolly. I am not amongst their number, but there *are* highwaymen. Do not forget that. Desperate men have been seen on the roads near Brigham Park and on the moors. Unscrupulous men, such as Mr Churchill, are always ready to prey on a woman such as yourself. Promise me you will not take any more unnecessary risks with that reputation, which I have defended tonight. Do I have your word?"

Catherine removed his coat from her shoulders and folded it over her arm before getting to her feet. She handed it to him and said, "Your request is not a difficult one to grant. After tonight, I have no desire to do anything at all that may be the cause of my ruin. You have my promise – my solemn word that I will not follow you or do anything else that may lead me into danger."

He slid his coat back on as he said, "Thank you, Miss Conolly. And now, I would be honoured to escort you from the drawing room. Are you ready?"

"I am ready, Your Grace. Thank you."

As he walked beside her through the hall, he made sure there was no one about who might see them. He assisted her as they ascended the stairs and past the landing, his arm at the ready should she falter in the darkness. At the top of the stairs, which led to the second floor, he stood like a sentry as she rushed to her room. Peering out the door of her chamber, she saw him still standing there, as motionless as stone.

He stood guard until she was safely inside her room, and then he turned and was gone, disappearing into the gloom of the hall.

How could I have been so wrong? Catherine wondered as she undressed in the cold. Sliding under the covers, she questioned how she had ever imagined he was a criminal. *Criminals do not defend a woman's honour* – she knew that to be true.

As she closed her eyes, she replayed the way he had threatened Mr Churchill and then cared for her so tenderly by the fireside. The duke had protected her and had struck that terrible Mr Churchill. The image of the gentleman coming to her rescue stayed with her, and she found herself unable to think of anything else. She thought of how dashing he had looked as he stood over Mr Churchill. Then her mind moved on to how charming his laugh was and his smile, until – at last – she fell asleep.

Chapter 15

The following day, Catherine rose at her usual time, as she did not want to provoke any suspicion in her maid or anyone else. She was so tired that her bones ached, but she had no desire to rest. Her curiosity and her apprehension were present in equal measure, as she went about her day – from a hazy beginning in the breakfast room to the drawing room later that morning. Her reason for being present from an early hour, was to ensure that, if there was the slightest hint of scandal, she would be among the first to hear of it.

It was something more than Mr Churchill's threats that gave her cause to be anxious. She had spent a large amount of her time lurking in rooms and sneaking around the house, listening to her uncle's private conversation and being alone with Mr Churchill and His Grace. If there was any hint of gossip circulating about her after last night, she would hear of it. She had exercised terrible judgement, and she had given even the staidest of gossipmongers a vast amount of fodder for any suspicions.

Regardless of playing her own part in contributing to any potential rumours, she half-expected that Mr Churchill would not keep his word to the duke. He struck her as the type of man who would take his revenge, if he was able to do so without any consequences. However, by the afternoon, she noticed that he *was* keeping his distance. He acknowledged her with a single nod, but that was all. He did not speak to her or to anyone about her. It was also becoming obvious to her that she was not the subject of conjecture or rumours. No one whispered about her, pointed at her, or treated her any differently that day than they had in the previous days – with one considerable and important exception.

Catherine noticed a change in the duke's demeanour, even if her uncle and mother did not. They spent the day frowning in her direction and scowling at every turn, whereas the duke exchanged knowing glances with Catherine, despite the lovely Miss Churchill never leaving his side. He remained cordial to the woman, whom he knew to be pursuing him, according to her brother. Miss Churchill seemed to be guarding him as if he was a prize, yet the duke smiled at Catherine occasionally, despite the prettier woman's presence. To her surprise, and just before the hunting party left that afternoon, he crossed the drawing room to speak to Catherine.

She remembered the conversation, despite the brevity of the discussion. The Duke of Rotherham waited until she was not in the company of Lady Frederica or her brother, the Earl of Burwickshire. He strode across the drawing room in a confident and proud manner, as befit the highest-ranking man in the room. When he stood directly before Catherine, he bowed and asked after her health.

"How are you, Miss Conolly?" he asked.

"I am as well as can be expected, Your Grace."

"I am delighted to hear that you are well. How fares your mother?"

"She is also well, and you, Sir?"

He answered that he was well and then wished her a good day. He then departed her company as quickly as he had arrived. He left her wondering why he would inquire about something as safe and dull as her health, when he could have discussed something more interesting. But she reasoned that, perhaps after last night, he truly was concerned about her health. When she thought back to this strange conversation, she realised that he may have been signalling to her without any outward indication to anyone else that he hoped that she had recovered from the night's adventures. She had no way of knowing whether she was correct in her assumption, but somehow, she imagined that she had correctly understood him. As she thought of the strange interaction a little longer, she decided that the duke may have not intended anything at all. He may have spoken to her about her health because he wished to be polite and to acknowledge the acquaintance, and nothing more. Still, try as she might, she could not forget how he had behaved in that same room, only the previous night.

Catherine gazed at the fireplace, and the memory of their private conversation came back to her. It was scandalous, but she had been alone with His Grace in this very room. His coat, which smelled of him, had been wrapped around her. She recalled the way he had spoken to her, and how he had made her promise that she would not sneak around the house late at night. His laugh echoed in her memory and she smiled.

How strange that one night, and one odd set of circumstances, could alter her impression of the gentleman and her own feelings for him. She had thought him handsome from the moment she had met him. His dark hair, grey eyes and pleasing features were hard to forget or ignore. Yet, after last night she regarded him as much more than an impressive aristocrat. She had seen a side to him that she did not dare to dream he possessed. She had heard his laugh: a rich baritone sound that was hard to forget. She smiled as she recalled the gentler side of the gentleman who had offered to build a fire so that she might stay warm.

Her thoughts were still of the duke as she settled into the pages of a novel. Catherine had no other means of distraction as she glanced towards the card table where Lady Frederica and her brother sat. They were playing cards again and she heard the cheerful sound of their laughter. She marvelled at how much they loved their games of chance and the amounts of money they both won and lost. In one hand of cards, she had observed Lady Frederica lose more money without a care, than Catherine had invested in all of her wardrobe!

"Catherine, would you come with me. I require a word with you." Her thoughts were interrupted by the viscount's voice, in an unfamiliar tone that suggested he was once again her benevolent benefactor.

She knew the reason for his pleasantness. While his guests were seated or standing nearby, he had to appear to be the very model of a generous and doting uncle. Her stomach turned in his presence. She had no wish to be polite to him, not when her anger boiled inside of her every time she looked at him. She felt indignation building every time he frowned at her.

Catherine glanced in her mother's direction and noted the woman's narrowed gaze. As a dutiful daughter, she swallowed her pride. "Is the drawing room not suitable, Uncle?"

He smiled but his eyes betrayed his displeasure at her answer. "No, my dear niece. I wish to have a word in private."

She had known that that was what he had meant but she could not resist a tiny moment of rebellion. Closing her novel, she rose and followed him from the room, out into the great hall. Catherine was terrified that he knew she had listened in on his conversation with Denton. Was he leading her to the study to upbraid and chide her?

Then he stopped abruptly. He did not make her walk that far to say what he wished to tell her. He pulled her into the far corner of the great hall and sneered at her. "Your continued lack of enthusiasm for securing the duke is disappointing. I see that today is no exception to your acceptance of failure."

"What failure would that be? Did you not observe that His Grace spoke to me today?"

"How could I observe such a trivial matter when I have observed Miss Churchill at his side, whereas you are not? If I did not know you to be determined in your efforts to save your family from starvation, I would think that you did not care to pursue the duke."

Catherine sighed. She was exhausted after the previous night's excitement and was still not in possession of the correct temperament to endure her uncle's relentless criticism. Staring at him, she thought of everything that made his manner repugnant. She despised the proud way that he held his head, the condescending tone of his voice, and the look of revulsion in his eyes as he glared at her. She wished she could tell him to leave her alone, and that she would be packed and gone this very day. But once again, she was compelled to bear his anger and his vile scheme. Despite his accusations, she did not want her family to be ruined.

"Uncle, I have tried to gain the duke's attention and I have succeeded. Whereas you consider his actions to be trivial and you claim you did not observe his speaking to me in the drawing room, I can assure you that he did. For a gentleman, such as His Grace, that must be some implication that he has noticed me."

Her uncle spat, "What care do I have if he speaks to you as he does to every other woman here at Brigham Park? A polite conversation hardly constitutes the efforts I have demanded of you. Your reluctance, or rather your negligence, has allowed another woman to presume upon the duke. If you were truly committed to this endeavour, I do not think you would have allowed such an occurrence."

"Are you referring to Miss Churchill? Uncle, how can I be blamed when you, yourself, invited a woman as charming as she is to Brigham Park?"

"You insolent, insignificant little worm. My invitation to the Churchills is none of your concern."

Catherine was no longer able to conceal her frustration. "She is my concern, as long as she prevents me from doing what I must, according to your directive."

"Miss Churchill should not be a deterrent to your task. She has endeared herself to the duke, despite being engaged to a gentleman from the Midlands. Her ambition to become a duchess is admirable – she has forgotten her engagement in the pursuit. Why can you not be similarly persuaded? Did you consider my threat, not to help your family, an idle one? Do you believe me to be sympathetic to your mother's pleas for help? I assure you, I meant what I said in our last conversation. Should you fail me, I will not give one penny to help your family."

Catherine wanted to reply, *you do not have a penny to spare*, at least not based on the conversation she had overheard, but she knew better than to do so. Instead, she said as calmly as she could, "I will do as you wish."

The words felt like poison in her mouth, but she was tired of listening to her uncle berate her. Her family was virtually destitute, and his own financial position was not much better. If he expected her to save *his* house for *him*, he was mistaken – there was nothing to be done. She was resigned to that terrible fate, so much so that she would not dream of shamelessly flirting with the Duke of Rotherham in order to change her circumstances.

She had discovered last night that the duke was an honourable man, after all. He did not deserve to be treated as a prize for a fortune hunter. If she must starve to preserve her dignity, then so be it – she would rather be poor than chase after the man who had saved her from harm. When she thought of him, she was astonished by how much her feelings towards him had changed. He was as noble and handsome as any hero in the novels she read. He even threatened to meet the villainous Mr Churchill in a duel for her! She would not be a willing part of any attempt to deceive or manipulate him for either her own or her uncle's gain.

"See that you do as I have asked, or the consequences will be terrible for you and your family," her uncle warned.

After Lord Wharton had left her in the hall, Catherine felt forlorn and melancholy. She wished she could be the kind of woman Miss Churchill obviously was – engaged to one gentleman but who did not let that liaison interfere with her ambition. If Catherine had been as cold and as unfeeling towards men as Miss Churchill was, then perhaps she would have had no reservations about ensnaring His Grace or any other man who was wealthy and had a title. However, she could not repay the Duke's kindness with an attempt to pull him into a match with a woman he did not love. Men such as the duke would never marry a woman without a dowry, connection, or title. Why humiliate herself, and embarrass him, by taking advantage of their new acquaintance and the turn of events? He had saved her from a dreadful fate – it would be unforgivable for her to presume upon the connection or his kindness.

She delayed returning to the drawing room, and, instead she slipped into a chair by the side of the enormous fireplace. The hall was quiet. The other guests were in the drawing room conversing or playing cards. Catherine welcomed the chance for solitude. She had much to think about and did not wish for distraction. As she stared into the blazing fire, watching the flames leaping high, she marvelled at the beauty of it. She sighed.

Sitting back in the chair, Catherine thought of her uncle's insistence on his demands. He was desperate. Her mother's frowns and scowls betrayed the same emotion. She regretted what was happening to her uncle and her cousin, Denton. She understood the helpless feeling that was caused by financial hardships. As much as she wished she could save Brigham Park for her cousin, and save her own family from ruin, she was not responsible for either turn of misfortune. Denton did not deserve to lose his birth right or his estate. Neither did her family deserve to be poor, but nothing that was honourable could change what was inevitable.

She was a young woman. She had inherited neither title nor rank, and she had no say in the financial decisions of her family. Her father had died greatly in debt. When she thought of how her mother and her uncle wanted to impose their hopes for the future upon her, she laughed at their folly in setting her to the task of securing a nobleman of the highest rank. They would see her in a loveless marriage to a man, such as His Grace, who would surely regret such a match, rather than do anything to either accept or change their own circumstances. She had read of such things in novels and blushed to consider them. She would not permit herself to think of it. She would not attempt to win him in a scandal or any other villainy.

Catherine also realised that her uncle was deceiving her mother as much as he was attempting to deceive her. Her uncle did not have the necessary means to support her family! Not when he was trying to save his own estate. The cost of this party, and the trappings of his wealth and title, must have been a vast sum. He had made a good display of it, but Catherine knew the truth. He needed money. So did her mother. Her mother was not going to receive *any* money, no matter how much she pleaded. With a chill, she realised that even if she was able to win the duke, her uncle had no intention of keeping his promises to her or her family. Her uncle had lied to her – he had lied to her mother. His deceit angered her, but it also made her feel vindicated in her having decided not to pursue the duke.

From the beginning, Catherine had been an unwilling participant in her uncle's scheme. She did not want to pursue the duke even when she had thought her uncle could help her family. Knowing that he was in a terrible predicament, and that his threats were all bluster, did nothing to alter her decision. If she did not want to pursue the duke then, she would not do it now. Not after last night.

It was more than the duke's heroics that had left Catherine feeling an immense gratitude. The Duke of Rotherham's nature was far warmer and more charming than she had presumed. If he wanted to pursue her either for friendship or something more, she would welcome it, but *she* would not presume upon the connection for one moment longer. She was not a woman who used her beauty as a weapon against a man who had come to her rescue. The duke was her champion and her hero, not a man who deserved to be hunted.

Catherine closed her eyes. She imagined herself as fashionably dressed as Miss Churchill, with the Duke of Rotherham at her side. In her fantasy, she was dressed in a white gown made of the finest material and it glittering in gold-hued sarsenet. Her hair was complemented by jewelled pins. The duke enjoyed her company, and she spoke as wittily and confidently as any of the other women at Brigham Park.

It was a delightful dream and one she fervently wished might come true, as she yawned and slowly fell asleep.

Chapter 16

Catherine's dream did not come true. She was not as fashionably dressed as Miss Churchill or Lady Frederica – and Catherine had come to the realisation that fashion and other trivial matters should be the least of her worries. Yet, a part of her dream did happen as she wished. The duke was at her side, speaking to her as if they had always been close acquaintances. Their secret seemed to have brought them closer together. They stood side-by-side in the drawing room that afternoon, enjoying each other's company, only hours after Catherine's delightful dream by the fireside in the hall.

"Your Grace, I want to thank you once more for coming to my rescue," she said to him as she watched Miss Churchill detained in conversation by the viscount.

To Catherine's surprise, the duke was not encumbered by any of the women of the party today, not even the lovely Miss Churchill. Miss Churchill looked longingly in the direction of the duke but appeared anxious about leaving her host. The viscount also glanced towards Catherine, but his expression was not anxious – it was steely.

"Miss Conolly, you have no need to thank me. What manner of gentleman would I have been to have allowed Mr Churchill to succeed in his endeavours? On the contrary, it is I who should thank you. I have not heard a single rumour circulating about last night. You seem adept at discretion ... a fine attribute and a rare one."

"Is it so rare to keep one's word?"

"It is rare in my experience."

With a smile, she said, "I have not been bothered by Mr Churchill. It would appear that he has heeded your words."

"Yes, it does appear that he has acted with great wisdom."

She laughed. "I am not sure we should think of him as wise. Bold and forward, most certainly, but undoubtedly not wise."

"He is also fortunate. If you had not insisted that he did not need to grovel before you, I would have made him do so. He did not deserve your generosity."

"No, he did not deserve it, but I am not cruel by nature."

"You are curious. I have never met a woman who has a more inquisitive nature than you do."

"If that is a compliment, I thank you."

"It *was* meant as a compliment," the duke said as Miss Churchill freed herself from the viscount. Catherine had been enjoying their conversation, and the few minutes she had alone with the duke. When she saw Miss Churchill striding purposefully towards them, Catherine said quietly, "I wonder if his sister will hold you responsible for injuring her brother."

"Perhaps she does not know of the incident. As I have said, he seems wise enough to heed my warnings."

Catherine saw Miss Churchill smiling pleasantly, but she observed her prey like a cat would, as she came to a halt in front of them. She did not acknowledge Catherine. Instead, she placed her hand on the duke's arm in a slightly inappropriate fashion.

"Your Grace, I regret I was unable to get away from our host," Miss Churchill began to the duke, "I have known him all of my life and he has never spoken so much to me as he has today. I was certain he would never find another person to distract him!"

The duke glanced at Catherine, and with a devilish smirk, he said, "Miss Conolly, do you often find your uncle to be loquacious?"

Catherine noticed the brief look of uncertainty that appeared on Miss Churchill's beautiful face. The woman actually appeared to be embarrassed, but only for a minute.

Her expression changed to arrogance. "Oh, Miss Conolly, I had forgotten that you were related to the viscount. I have no doubt that it is a common mistake made by many of the other guests." Miss Churchill held her head high as she spoke, appearing rather pleased with herself. "My brother is playing cards – why not keep him company? I am certain he would welcome it."

"Miss Churchill, I cannot part with Miss Conolly at present," the duke jumped in. "Unless, of course, she wishes to leave my company. She and I were discussing Mr Shelley's recent works. I found her opinion on the matter to be refreshing."

"How drab a subject," Miss Churchill complained in a childish voice. "Shall we not discuss something livelier, such as the ball tomorrow evening?"

Catherine had quite forgotten about the ball, the event that signalled the end of the party, and therefore also signalled the last night she would be able to spend in the company of the duke. This reminder nearly eclipsed the small lie that the duke had told Miss Churchill. Catherine watched as Miss Churchill appeared flustered, as she realised that she was not in control of the situation at the moment.

"If you wish to discuss the ball, I have no wish to bore you with our conversation. Perhaps the other ladies would find the ball a far more appealing subject?" he offered with a smile.

Miss Churchill looked at Catherine aghast. "You are discussing Shelley? How interesting that your family can afford books, at the expense of your wardrobe."

The insult was not subtle. Still, Catherine had no wish to spar with Miss Churchill and she replied, "It is true, my family cannot afford a better wardrobe for me. However, fashion and beauty are not eternal, whereas a good book and a well-written verse are time-less. Why waste money on trivial concerns when the value of knowledge is far above wealth?"

Miss Churchill appeared as smug in defeat as she did at any other time.

"Miss Churchill, you are far too beautiful and fashionable to find our conversation to have any merit." The duke broke the silence. "It pains me to think of you forced to endure the dullness of it. If you will permit us a few moments to finish our discourse, I promise that I will discuss the ball, as you wish."

Catherine was astonished that His Grace was dismissing Miss Churchill politely and without a hint of malevolence. She wanted to applaud him, but she refrained from any obvious signs of delight as she smiled serenely at Miss Churchill.

With a haughty tone, Miss Churchill remarked, "Your Grace is correct, no woman of *accomplishment* or *worth* would find books and literature to be a fascinating subject. I venture the topic appeals only to governesses and tutors or their sort. I am grateful that you have saved me from such a tedious discussion."

With a smile at the duke and a glare in the direction of Catherine, Miss Churchill walked away. The duke leaned over slightly and whispered, "Tell me, do you know Shelley? I would hate to think of myself as a man capable of deceit."

"Shelley? I do know of his work and I heartily approve of him. After all, I have been likened to governesses and tutors and their sort. I should consider my knowledge of Shelley and all literature to recommend me to an employer."

"Miss Conolly? How can you hope to be a governess? With your extraordinary talent for disregarding the rules of society and your independence, what sort of model would you be to young minds?" The duke speculated.

"I should strive to be less independent, I suppose." She smiled.

"I think you will find the endeavour to be a dismal failure. I do not mean to insult you by that sentiment, but you are unlike any woman I have known. I cannot imagine you confined by the strict rules that a governess must follow. Not a woman of your intelligence and your beauty!"

Catherine was astonished. Did he say that she was intelligent and beautiful? She did not know how to remark upon his statement, so she stood quite speechless at his side.

"Shall we talk of Shelley, so I am not proved to be a dreadful liar?"

Catherine was reeling from his compliment, nearly as much as she was by how politely he had dispatched Miss Churchill.

"We shall speak of Shelley, but I must confess that I may not be knowledgeable of his most recent works. I am embarrassed to admit that I have not had the necessary means to collect the contemporary works of the more modern writers."

"No matter – we shall speak of his talent and the works that are known to you, if that suits you. I would suggest that we speak of the novels you favour, but I do not read them. I wonder... is it in those same novels you read that led you to your surveillance of me when you thought me to be the highwayman?"

"You consider that I have been influenced by the stories I have read?"

"I do believe it to be so. It seems to me you were influenced by the adventures of the characters and their heroics, which must surely have led you to pursue me without fear of consequence. I know you have an interest in novels, and you cannot tell me otherwise, even if the books you collected from the viscount's library were hardly sensational."

"My interests are varied. I enjoy reading novels for the thrilling stories, as I find my own life to be tedious, at times. However, I am not solely devoted to contemporary books, many of which may be considered sensational. I also study history and philosophy and find enjoyment in both subjects."

"Did you enjoy the *History of Yorkshire*?"

"You recall the book, Sir? I am astonished that you remember it so well."

He smiled at her as he said, "I recall a great many things, Miss Conolly. I do not wish to catalogue them at present, as I fear our time has come to a close. I gave my word to Miss Churchill, and despite the difficulties between myself and her brother, I intend to keep my word. Perhaps you would care to join us? We may discuss the ball or any number of other suitably predictable subjects."

Catherine saw Miss Churchill staring at the duke from the other side of the room, looking petulant. Catherine understood the duke's attention was required by Miss Churchill and the other people in the drawing room, and that their pleasant conversation had come to an end.

"I appreciate your asking, but I shall take my leave for another distraction. I thank you for the conversation – it has been enjoyable."

"It has been for me as well." He paused for a second. "I would not permit Miss Churchill's ill-mannered ways to get the better of you. She may think much of herself, but she is the epitome of what I have come to expect from her class. As I have encouraged the acquaintance, I have no wish to embarrass her." Just as Catherine was curtseying, she heard him say. "Miss Conolly, I would like to continue our talk some other time, after dinner perhaps?"

Catherine was jubilant, but she hid it well. Willing herself to remain composed, she concealed her excitement. "Shall we meet in the drawing room?"

"I prefer the library. We may speak as we wish and will not be disturbed by more than a few men who seek solace and quiet amongst the books."

"Then we shall meet in the library."

"Until then." He bowed.

As she walked away, the duke re-joined the dreadful Miss Churchill. The woman was now gloating as the duke stood by her side.

Catherine was not certain how she should feel about their short but wonderful conversation. He wanted to meet her again! The moment Catherine left the duke's company, she had felt the weight of someone's gaze upon her. She felt innately that she was being watched. She glanced around the crowded room. Many women were looking at her, amongst them, her own mother, who was seated in the company of a small circle of older women and who was looking in her direction – and she was smiling.

Chapter 17

Catherine was bitterly disappointed but there was nothing to be done.

Nothing at all!

Her mother, who had seemed to be thrilled at seeing Catherine and the duke together, had ruined Catherine's nascent friendship with His Grace. Why did her friendship with him have to end as soon as it had? Oh, how she regretted her mother's terrible blunder.

When she thought of the incident that had occurred yesterday evening, she mused on the irony that her chances of becoming better acquainted with the duke had been dashed to bits by her mother, of all people! She would not have been surprised if it had been Mr Churchill or his sister, or even the viscount himself, who were to blame for the calamity, but her mother? It was almost inconceivable. After all, her mother was the same woman who had insisted they come to Brigham Park and who had demanded that Catherine comply with her uncle's scheme.

But indeed, she *had* ruined Catherine's budding friendship with His Grace – broken and destroyed it! The Duke of Rotherham was no longer amiable to Catherine, nor was he speaking to her.

Catherine was lying shut away in her room, on her bed, an hour before the ball was to begin. She was refusing to dress or to have her hair styled for the ball. Instead of the night she had been anticipating, filled with dancing and merriment, she now dreaded going downstairs and facing the duke. She cringed when she recalled the incident that had so destroyed the duke's opinion of her. Catherine had not been able to escape it, and it played over and over again in her mind. How she wished it had never happened! How she wished she was able to change it, but she could not. It had happened and it had altered the duke's feelings remarkably.

Catherine recalled, with perfect clarity, how it had all transpired. She and the duke had just left the library the previous evening. It was after dinner. He had stayed in the dining room with the other gentlemen as was expected. An hour later, he had emerged and made his way to the library to meet up with Catherine, where she was sitting by the fireside, a book of Shelley's poetry in her lap. The duke was accompanied by another man, an older gentleman whom Catherine assumed was not interested in the parlour games and cards of the drawing room. With the older gentleman present, a knight she recalled, she and the duke were not alone, so they were able to avoid any hint of scandal.

How happy she had been when the duke had greeted her, and then sat across from her as if they had always sat together by the fireside. They talked for half an hour or more. Catherine had lost track of the time and all else in his presence. They laughed and shared stories of their lives. In the conversation, Catherine watched as the duke became a different person. Gone were the stiff aristocratic manners and the polite discourse. Without an audience of other nobles around him, he spoke to her as though they were dear friends. He treated her as a lady – he smiled, laughed and made her feel at ease. How delightful it had been, to be with a gentleman who asked her about her thoughts and opinions and was sincerely interested in her answers. The duke treated her as if she were a person who mattered, who was worthy of admiration – not because of a family name or a title, but simply because of who she was as a person. The way he treated her was unlike anything she had ever felt before, and it was a feeling she wished to have once again – but now that would never be.

That happy memory would remain nothing more than that: a small part of her life forever consigned to be a sad reminder that she had hoped and striven far above her station. Catherine had not dreamt of marrying the duke; however, she did want him to admire her, and to regard her as a friend. Now, he had turned against her and she could not console herself.

Catherine was sitting beside His Grace, and they were laughing about a funny anecdote he had shared about his youth, something about a prank he had played on a cruel tutor, as she recalled. They were having a marvellous time, as they left the library together and strolled into the drawing room. There, they came upon her mother speaking rather loudly to one of her companions.

Catherine shook her head as she recalled her mother's words, said in a loud tone of voice, which reverberated far too widely. Lady Conolly, her back turned to the door, was addressing an older woman in an enormous turban with several peacock feathers in her hair.

"My dear, I tell you my daughter has performed as perfectly as any actor on a stage. She has played her role to perfection and as a result, she has him in her grasp."

"Whomever can you mean? Not His Grace the Duke of Rotherham, the legendary highness of the dark moors?" the befeathered woman ventured.

"Yes, indeed! It is *him* of whom I am speaking. Catherine would have no other man from the very start. She has always been ambitious ... an admirable trait in one so young. With her beauty, nobody else but a duke or some other wealthy gentleman would do. She has succeeded in her task and we shall be all the better for it. I am sure she will be the Duchess of Rotherham by spring. All she requires is his proposal! He will ask for her hand any day now – have you seen how he adores her? He is enraptured, I tell you."

Catherine stood beside the duke, praying that he had not overheard the same dreadful conversation. Her mother was boasting and bragging about how Catherine had managed to enrapture the duke, but nothing could be farther from the truth.

By the time her mother came to the awful realisation that the Duke of Rotherham and Catherine were standing behind her, it was far too late to change what had been said. Her words had been overheard. The duke was no longer laughing nor was he smiling. With a sudden chill that Catherine could swear she felt, he frowned and then turned to her as he said simply, "If you will excuse me."

He did not say anything else to her or anyone as he left the drawing room.

Catherine stood in a state of near shock, and her mother turned pale as white muslin. Catherine wanted to run after him, to tell him that her mother was wrong, but she could not bring herself to face him. How could she? Her mother was telling the truth, even if she had worded it in such an awful way. Catherine *had* been tasked with marrying no other man but him, even though she did not pursue him because her uncle and her mother wished it.

Her face flushed red and tears welled in her eyes. She stood, staring at her mother and was unable to speak for what seemed many minutes. She watched her mother slowly realise the repercussions of her thoughtless bragging. The last words she heard her mother mumble that night were an apology as Catherine left the drawing room and rushed up the stairs into her own bedchamber, where she fell onto the bed and wept.

Oh, the look he had given her!

Ever since, it had been no better. He hardly looked at her, he did not speak to her, and he did not give her even the slightest opportunity to offer an explanation for her mother's ill-timed comments. He treated her as he had done before – with disregard. Miss Churchill, on the other hand, did not ignore Catherine. She gloated from her position of prominence at the duke's side. Catherine recalled Miss Churchill's victorious looks in her direction as she lay on her bed crying and thinking about her flight up the stairs to her room.

As the musicians arrived and the ballroom opened up to the guests, Catherine could no longer endure his obvious eschewal of her, or her mother's numerous apologies. She wished to stay in her room. She heard the first notes struck by the musicians. The ball was beginning, but she could not bring herself to attend. Even if that meant she would never see His Grace again. Weeping into a pillow, Catherine barely heard the insistent knock at the door. She did not want to see or speak to anyone, but the door opened and shut, and then she heard a familiar voice.

"Miss, I know I may lose my position for not doing what you told me to do, but I cannot bear to see you locking yourself up here and missing the ball. It would not be right. You have to go to the ball — you cannot miss it!" Bess exclaimed.

"Yes, I can miss it and I will, if I choose," Catherine said without looking up.

"No — it would not be proper for a woman such as you to not attend the ball? I have never heard of such a thing! Come along and I will fix your hair."

"Bess, bring me a cup of tea if you want to, but that is all I require," Catherine said as she sat up and stared at the maid who was holding something shimmery and cream-coloured. Catherine gestured to it. "What are you holding in your hands?"

"Miss, this dress I have here? This is for you."

"But ... it is not a dress I own."

"This dress is a gift from Lady Frederica. I have spent the last few days altering it to fit you. You have to wear it — you have to go to the ball."

Catherine was almost speechless. "Lady Frederica sent that to me? It is ... beautiful. And you did that for me? If I was not already weeping, I would cry from gratitude."

"Stop crying, Miss. The ball has begun. We don't have much time to make you presentable!" Bess exclaimed as Catherine stood and wiped her face.

She did not feel like going downstairs to see a ballroom full of people from the party, as well as the local gentry, but she could not refuse Lady Frederica's generous gift, nor could she ignore the hours of work that Bess had put into making a gown that had been tailored for Lady Frederica's ample figure, to fit Catherine's petite one. As Bess immediately went to work, she reasoned that she could stay at the ball for a few minutes, long enough to express her gratitude to Lady Frederica.

An hour later, Catherine stood in front of the dressing table. She looked regal as Bess admired her work. The gown was still a little loose in places, but Bess's skill with a needle could not be disputed. The gown was exquisite. It was a shimmering blue colour and was lined with ribbons in ivory-and-gold hues. The colour complemented Catherine's fair skin and chestnut hair, which was styled in a simple but elegant bun. Bess had wound a thin gold ribbon through Catherine's tresses which looked elegant. In an hour, Bess had made Catherine into the very image of a high-born lady. As she admired her reflection, she was overwhelmed by the efforts of the maid.

Catherine's eyes filled with tears of joy. Still, she managed to smile for the maid. "Bess, what skill you possess. This gown and my hair … make me look as though I am a countess."

"That was my wish. If I may be so bold as to repeat her ladyship's wishes. She swore me to secrecy about this gown. If I were to wager, I would say she wanted you to look just like the other fine ladies here at Brigham Park."

"How can I ever repay her or you? You must have spent hours altering this dress to fit me."

"I did not mind the work," Bess said proudly. "I like sewing."

"Bess, if I ever become a wealthy woman, I promise I will hire you as my maid without hesitation."

"Thank you, Miss. In this dress, and with the way you look, I'm sure you will be engaged by the end of the night!"

Catherine did not have the heart to tell Bess that the chances of her becoming engaged that night (or ever) were very low. After Catherine returned home, she faced a future that would surely see her leaving to seek work as a governess or a companion. She did not wish to destroy Bess's hopes. The young woman who had worked so diligently on the ballgown, was staring at her with an optimistic expression on her face.

"You are beautiful, Miss. You look like a proper lady!" Bess exclaimed as Catherine thanked her once more and left the safety of the bedroom.

With every step down the corridor, the music from downstairs echoed through the house. It grew louder as she came to the stairs. Standing at the top of the staircase, she looked at the landing and sighed. She was standing where His Grace had stood the night he had rescued her from Mr Churchill. Thinking about the moment he had displayed his courage helped her to descend the steps. She knew that if she had stayed hidden in her room, she would have regretted her cowardice for the rest of her life. She was careful not to step on the gown, which was slightly longer than her own dresses. With every step, she thought of His Grace. Tonight would be the last chance she would have to explain everything to him. She would find the duke and speak to him, even if he had no wish to hear her. What did she care if there were consequences? Her uncle was facing ruin, her own family was poor already, so what did it matter if she risked her good name or her reputation? *She would never see anyone here at Brigham Park again.* The thought emboldened her, so she held her head high and stepped from the staircase to the great hall.

The very first thing she did was seek out Lady Frederica and her brother. Thanking them both for their friendship and the gift of the dress, Catherine felt much better. She would miss them both, and she was buoyed by their promises to write to her. One day in the future, Lady Frederica promised she would invite Catherine to come to their estate. It was a noble gesture and one that would have delighted Catherine even more had she not been consumed by her purpose. She had to find the duke and speak to him, regardless of his reaction. Just as Catherine was searching the room, Lady Frederica accepted the invitation of a dashing young man to dance, and Catherine accepted the same request from the Earl of Burwickshire, who was as dear to her as a good friend. As they danced, she glanced around the ballroom and her eyes found the duke. Miss Churchill was on his arm. She was dressed in a deep-crimson gown. The colour was as stunning as her complexion, which seemed rosier given the hue of her dress. Regardless of Catherine's opinion of Miss Churchill, she was stunning, and Catherine had to admit that they were the most handsome couple in the ballroom.

As soon as the dance ended, Catherine took a long, deep breath. She knew that the time had come, and she thanked her partner for the dance. She could not wait any longer to speak to the duke. She was not willing to spend her life regretting her decision because of cowardice. She set her sights on the duke, as she walked past her uncle, with a determined look in her eyes. The latter glowered at her from a distance while her mother appeared stricken.

Miss Churchill was hanging onto the duke's arm as if she were already his wife. She drew closer to His Grace, with the smile of triumph of an almost-duchess, as she saw Catherine approaching. This time, Catherine did not feel as plain as she had the first time she was introduced to him. In her new gown, she was dressed as handsomely as any other woman in the ballroom. She was lacking the jewels of the wealthier set, but her clothes and her beauty were equal (or even superior) to any woman in the room. As she walked across the floor, she felt the admiring looks of the young men, and many women stared at her in silent approval. She hoped that the duke would be struck by her appearance tonight.

"Is that not the poor niece of the viscount? Has he clothed her in something borrowed, so she does not disgrace him on this fine evening?" Miss Churchill said to a companion as she sneered in the direction of Catherine.

Catherine overheard but did not reply to the slight. Her concentration was fixed on the duke, who looked handsome tonight. With his steel-grey eyes and thick, wavy hair, he was equally as remarkable in his appearance as he was in his choice of coat and breeches. Both were dark and sombre but tailored to exacting standards and which fit his muscular built to perfection. He did not smile as she walked towards him. His gaze was cool. Even though she was trembling inside, she managed to keep her voice steady.

"Your Grace, forgive the intrusion. I would like to speak to you."

"What could you have to say to him that he would find interesting?" Miss Churchill interrupted. "Run along to your books, if you are in need of distraction."

"I am sure His Grace can answer the question himself," Catherine replied.

"What do you wish to say to me?" The duke spoke to Catherine without a trace of warmth in his voice.

Catherine knew that she was being watched and listened to by almost everybody in the room. She had no desire to embarrass herself or the duke, but she had to speak to him alone. Choosing her words carefully, she said, "Sir, I have given you my opinion of Mr Shelley but not of Lord Byron."

Miss Churchill laughed. "Oh, my, how dull. You cannot think he would wish to discuss something as trivial as literature at a ball?"

The duke stared at her. His gaze remained narrowed, but she saw something unreadable in his expression. She waited for his rebuke, but it did not come. Instead, he said, "You may have a short audience, Miss Conolly, even though this subject no longer holds any interest for me."

Catherine understood what he implied but it did not deter her. She walked at his side as he strode purposively and quickly from the ballroom into the hall. There were other guests gathered in the hall, but he managed to find a quiet alcove by the fireplace. There, he turned to speak to her. "I cannot imagine what possessed you to embarrass me and yourself in the ballroom. I will not insult you openly, but I find your lack of decorum a reminder of your humble origins."

Catherine felt as if he had physically struck her. His words were cutting and painful and she was not prepared for their viciousness. Tears came to her eyes, but she fought them back as she gathered her strength and said, "I may deserve your harsh words and your cruelty, but I promise not to waste your time any longer than I must."

"What do you have to say to me that you think would interest me? I know we did not come here for a discussion about the literature of Byron," he said without a hint of warmth.

"Correct, Sir. That is not the reason why I wanted to speak to you. I am here about my mother. It is impossible that you did not hear her boasts about you and me."

"I heard them. I *was* astonished ... but I should not have been. Why should you be different from every other woman I have met? I am not married, nor am I engaged. There is a reason why I have not chosen a wife. I have yet to find one amongst your sex who is trust-worthy and honest, and who does not seek me for my title and my fortune."

"I did not seek you for anything–"

"Oh, you did not? Is this the acting your mother was so proud of? Are you playing the role of a despairing young woman so I shall lis-ten to you and have sympathy?"

"I play no role. I am as you see me. I cannot be blamed for my mother's careless words or her empty dreams for my future. My fam-ily faces ruin. If my mother dreams that I will save the family, then how am *I* to stop her?" Catherine asked, admitting the truth of her circumstances.

"You confess that you did seek me for my fortune. Are you so bra-zen as to believe your beauty and charm have won me?"

"I am not brazen ... and I am not a fortune seeker. If I were such a woman, would I not have orchestrated a scandal to trap you in a matter of dishonour? Did I not have ample opportunity to appeal to my uncle that you had taken advantage of me, luring me away from my bed late at night? If that was not scandalous enough, what about your mysterious errands? Did anyone hear of them?"

There was a moment of silence.

"I cannot deny that you have shown a remarkable strength of character for a woman. But your mother may have been telling the truth. You may have engineered my trust as part of your scheme to entrap me."

"And you may be as villainous as Mr Churchill or the highwayman? You left Brigham Park on the night there was an attack. I thought it once, and before the end of my stay, I may think it again. Yet, I did not summon the magistrate or endanger you by spreading gossip."

He exhaled loudly as he leaned in close to her and said, "Your arguments are compelling – but they are useless. I know the truth about you and your uncle. Shall I recount what I know, to show you that your arguments are hopeless?"

Catherine swallowed, as her mind raced. "I have nothing to conceal from you, nothing at all."

"I think you do. In a house such as Brigham Park, one hears many things. My valet is a man who is astute at learning whatever he wishes from the other servants. Shall I tell you of a secret that is whispered amongst them?"

He glared at Catherine who moved her head up and down once.

"Your uncle is not as rich as he seems. In fact, his situation is so dire that he will lose this house and his property. You have been summoned here to be a pawn in his game. Your reward is a title and my wealth with the outcome that your family will no longer have to face humiliation and ruin."

"Please—" Catherine wanted to reply, but he did not let her speak.

"I knew this about you when we were introduced, so I chose to keep you at a distance. I was unable to do as I wished when you proved to be far too inquisitive about my affairs and then, to make matters worse, you also managed to endanger yourself with Mr Churchill."

"I am not a pawn. It is true that my uncle is ruined and so is my family, but I was *not* doing as I was asked to do ... please believe me," she said, desperate for him to listen to her.

"I want to believe you, but I cannot. How could I be so foolish as to believe a word you say? You endear yourself to me by keeping my secret. You put yourself in harm's way to illicit my help and then I decide, against my better judgement, to alter my opinion of you. I was prepared to alter it further in your favour until your mother confirmed the worst of my suspicions about you. I dare not think of how close you were to succeeding in your scheme, had we not happened upon her that evening."

Catherine could feel her heart pounding wildly under the gossamer fabric of Lady Frederica's gown. She was close to fainting. He was telling her that he cared about her, was he not?

"Sir, I am not a willing pawn of my uncle. I do not know what to say to make you believe me. Unfortunately, I do not see any way to prove my genuine intentions. What I said to you, and how I acted around you ... what I felt was *all* sincere."

He stared at her. His face was near hers as he leaned in closer, so close that she could see all the different shades of grey in his eyes. For a moment he held still. Catherine braced herself for what she hoped would be a statement of understanding, kind words of apology, or, she gasped – a kiss.

Just when Catherine began to close her eyes, he spoke up.

"Miss Conolly, your scheme has ended in failure. I will not be led astray by either your handsome countenance or your intellect. I regret that I permitted myself to be swayed by you and your charm, but that is a mistake I shall not make again. If you have nothing left to say to me, I will take my leave of you. I am expected back in the ballroom."

His words stung her once again. She did not have anything else to say to him. He turned, but then he seemed to recall something further and he spun back around and faced her.

"Your uncle's schemes have come to naught, Miss Conolly. Lord Wharton will lose Brigham Park. He will sell his property and I shall buy it. It will give me great pleasure to evict him from this house, knowing that he plotted against me. I bid you good night."

With that, the Duke of Rotherham walked away.

This time, he did not turn around. He was gone, and with him, he took any feelings she harboured for him in her heart. Catherine leaned against a nearby chair, and held on to it, willing herself not to faint. Brigham Park would be lost to her uncle and her family could not be saved. That was dreadful news, but it was nothing compared to the cold panic she felt deep inside.

He loathed her.

He never wanted to see her again and that hurt far worse than any nightmare of poverty that she faced. How was she supposed to live, now that she had tasted the first stirrings of love and been denied so cruelly?

As tears fell down her face, she found the strength to leave the hall and to bid farewell to Brigham Park and the dark moors.

Chapter 18

Catherine frowned as she stood in a small, drably furnished bedroom in a narrow grey stone townhouse in London. The house, like the bedroom she now occupied, was not fashionable, nor was it luxurious. It was a plain, unremarkable residence located several blocks from the more stylish district of Mayfair. Yet, there was one advantage. Although this house was not located in the most enviable of neighbourhoods, it was still considered completely suitable, and therefore acceptable for the lowest ranks amongst society: the baronets, knights, and landed gentry who were not quite as wealthy or as well-connected as other peers of the realm.

Inside the drab little house, all of the rooms were furnished economically. Only the drawing room boasted luxurious items on display. Catherine's room was not much better than the servants' quarters at her family's estate, which had been leased in the new year.

But none of that mattered much to Catherine. Neither did she fret about her family's recent financial downturn, the address of her home, nor her recent fall farther down the ranks of society. She faced a far more pressing matter at that moment. An invitation to Almack's, and the dress she held in her hands.

The blue- and cream-coloured dress was the only frock she owned that would be fashionable enough for Almack's. She touched the filmy and expensive fabric. Memories as sharp and painful as if she was reliving them, overwhelmed her. The dress was more than just a dress – it was a reminder of one of the worst nights of her life. Smoothing the fabric with her fingers, she recalled with perfect clarity that she had worn that dress months ago to a ball attended by some of the highest peers in society. It was the last time she had seen *him*.

Today, on a day in early spring, her only companion was an inquisitive red-headed woman. The woman in possession of such a stunning shade of red hair, was Miss Patience Smyth, governess to Catherine's sister, Jane. She was also Catherine's dear friend. Patience gave her opinion of the dress without reservation. "Oh, my, that is a lovely gown. I have never seen anything as beautiful."

"It is lovely … but I cannot wear it." Catherine sighed.

"Oh, and why is that? Is it the style? I can see that it is a ballgown. Do you think it would be considered out of place at Almack's? Forgive me, for as you well know, I do not concern myself with such things."

"No, it is stylish. At least it was this past autumn. It is not the style that I object to. A ballgown should be appropriate for Almack's. There *is* dancing, after all."

"Well, I see … but what can be the cause of your hesitation? If you have been invited to Almack's, you cannot wear anything less than something splendid. I do not mean to cause offence or to insult you, since your family employs me, but I do not think you possess another dress equal to the company who will surely be at that venerable club. I have seen your wardrobe, and this is truly the only available dress for such an occasion."

Catherine looked at her friend, who was an honest woman, and nodded. Ordinarily, she would not have been permitted to ally herself with a woman who was employed as a governess, but since the recent tumble of her own family's status in society, she did not think such decorum applied any longer. Catherine did not care who knew of it – not when her own prospects looked so dismal. She had already decided that if she was not married by the end of the season, she would seek to work as a governess herself.

"I have no reason to grumble, do I? I should be excited to accept the invitation to Almack's … but the truth, dear Patience, is that I do not care to go."

Catherine's tone sounded hushed, as if she had confessed to some terrible crime. Speaking of an invitation to Almack's was something often done in reverent tones. The invitation was considered almost sacred. It was rare to receive one, since there were a limited number of members and even fewer people were invited to the hallowed halls of the exclusive club. For a woman such as Catherine, who boasted barely any rank and was largely considered unfashionable because of her impoverished circumstances, an invitation to Almack's was nearly as unbelievable as if she had suddenly been declared queen! She knew people who would gladly accept an invitation to accompany the devil himself, if it meant gaining entry into Almack's.

"Have I shocked you?" she asked Patience.

"No, you have not shocked me. On the contrary. If *I* were to receive an invitation to Almack's, I, too, should hesitate to accept. What business does someone such as me, a governess, have to go to a place frequented by the ton and their like?"

"Patience, I am similarly inclined. I would have declined the invitation but did not because of the person who sent it. My cousin, Denton Keeling, has asked me to accompany him, for a reason I cannot presume. I must go, if for no other reason than to ascertain his reason for re-acquainting himself with me in such a public manner."

"Then you *must* wear this dress. What choice do you have?" declared Patience.

"Regrettably, I have no other course. Perhaps this dress will bring me far better luck than it did the last time I wore it," fretted Catherine.

Patience replied brightly, "If it does not bring you good luck, you can always give it to me. I should not hesitate to wear it, if only I had some reason to don such a dress."

"I wish you will one day, my dear Patience."

Despite her numerous bad feelings about wearing the exquisite dress, Catherine could find no real reason not to do so. She was going to Almack's. She had her own family name to consider – not that the Conolly's were highly thought of these days. Her brother Henry had valiantly managed to retain ownership of the estate, but he had had no choice but to lease the house to a merchant, Mr Ulysses Grisham. There was the consolation, at least, that the property was saved, however Catherine still felt the pain of losing her home. Mr Grisham was an amiable man. His wife and his children were charming. Yet her opinion of them did little to alleviate the pain of being separated from the house and grounds she adored and the idyllic country setting. Then there was the matter of their current predicament. With their estate leased, they were compelled to live in London all year as residents and not as the other landed families, who remained in town for the social season only. Her brother felt the removal from the estate keenly, but he promised Catherine that the leasing arrangements were a temporary measure only. In a few years' time, they would return to their country house, their debts paid. His words were meant to be comforting, but they gave her little cause to be hopeful.

But that was not a matter for worrying about now, not when Catherine had less than two hours in which to dress, before her cousin Denton arrived to collect her.

It was curious that he had invited her (or even acknowledged her at all) after the disastrous hunting party. It was at the end of that occasion that her uncle had declared her endeavour to be a failure and had sent her mother and her away with the assurance that he wished never to see either of them again. At her uncle's insistence, she and her family were to be forever relegated to the status of distant and impoverished relations, undeserving of his acknowledgement or his financial assistance. The day they left Brigham Park had been the beginning of the terrible shift in their fortunes.

In London, they were now viewed as a curiosity, by some. They occupied a particular level of society, but they were without the means to make any connections or to keep the company of those who shared their rank but not their misfortune. Amongst their own set, invitations to tea or dinner were few, and of those, only the connections that were either too wealthy or too powerful to care for the opinions of society, seemed to notice the Conollys at all.

Lady Frederica and her brother were kind and compassionate people, and they invited Catherine to tea on occasion. There was also a polite invitation from the family of a knight who lived nearby, and of course, the landowner and his wife who, like the Conollys, were neither wealthy nor middle class, but occupied the precarious position of being amongst society – but not actually considered to have any true status. And so, Catherine and her family continued with a reduced staff. The governess was required for her dear sister Jane, but lady's maids were not a necessity, as the family socialised so rarely.

For a woman in her current state, an invitation to Almack's was truly an oddity, and one Catherine hoped her cousin would explain when he arrived. She did not have to wait long. At precisely the time stated on the invitation, Denton arrived at the family's new residence, which sat in a block of similarly plain residences. Despite her reservations regarding her cousin, Catherine was excited to meet him in the drawing room. After a friendly welcome, she agreed to spend an evening at Almack's in his company.

Catherine's mother had been astonished when the invitation had arrived. Catherine knew that the woman had sent letters to her brother, since their demise, and also that those letters had gone unanswered. For Denton to invite Catherine to accompany him, to spend an evening at London's most fashionable club, was almost not to be believed, until he actually arrived. Her mother's face was a picture of puzzlement and thinly veiled hope, as Catherine bid her farewell. However, as she left her modest home, Catherine was apprehensive. She did not understand what her cousin hoped to achieve, but she was certain he would soon reveal his scheme.

She was not disappointed.

Chapter 19

Denton Keeling looked every bit the fashionable gentleman that Catherine knew him to be, as he escorted her to his carriage. They settled into the carriage and he rapped on the ceiling to signal to the driver that the occupants were safely inside and seated.

The first five minutes of the journey to the venerated address of Almack's, on King Street, was spent in polite chatter. Denton inquired about her family, while she asked about his father and his brother, without a hint of malice. Once the pleasantries had been properly addressed, Catherine studied her cousin, willing herself to wait patiently for the explanation that must be forthcoming. The sound of the horse's hooves on the road was the only sound she heard, until Denton cleared his throat. At first, he looked a little sheepish, and then he proceeded to do something that she would not have expected a Keeling to be capable of. He offered what seemed to be a genuine apology.

"Catherine, I would like to thank you for accompanying me tonight. On behalf of my family, and my father, I pray you will find it in your heart to forgive the wrong that has been done to you. It is a wrong that I wish to make right."

Catherine saw Denton's expression in the carriage, illuminated by the faint lantern light. It was sincere.

She had never told him that she had overheard the conversation between his father and him, that fateful evening when he learned of his father's scheme to save their estate.

Catherine did not intend to bring up past matters, so she replied, "There is no need for you to apologise."

"I am ashamed by my father's attempts to involve you in his plans to ally with the Duke of Rotherham. I am ashamed by his ill treatment of your mother and your family during this trying time. I also know of the uncertainty that you have faced. I do not wish to speak of it, but I should tell you, as I know you to be a trustworthy person. You know the fortune of the Keelings was spent and that we faced selling Brigham Park. However, I insisted we pursue a rather risky investment, which has proven profitable. I am glad to report that we are no longer in any danger of losing our estate, but I regret that the investment did not become profitable until after your arrival in London."

Catherine was not prepared for her cousin's candour.

"Has your father sent you to apologise and to offer assistance?" she asked.

Denton shook his head as he replied, "No, he has not, I am sad to say. In fact, he has no knowledge that I have contacted you ... nor does he know that I wish to help you when I become viscount. As it stands, I am not able to do as much as I would like to do, however, I wish to do what I am able to – with your permission, of course."

"Is that the reason why you have invited me to join you at Almack's? Is it prudent that you should be seen in my company in such a fashionable and public place?"

"I care not for the opinion of anyone who would consider a cousin contemptible for doing his duty by his family. If I had been more courageous earlier, I would have righted this wrong at the hunting party. Instead, I have waited to learn of the outcome of my own future – selfishly, I suppose. Now I wish to look to you and to discuss what is to become of the Conollys."

"By securing an evening's invitation to Almack's? I pray that you will understand my reticence in the matter. My confidence in your family's assistance to myself has been sorely eroded. I have never known you to be duplicitous, so I have no reason to suspect that you do not speak sincerely, but I must confess that I am curious what you could hope to achieve by an evening of cards and dancing."

Her cousin smiled. It was a perfectly charming smile that served to make her even more curious and quite frankly, slightly anxious.

"Denton, I do wish you would tell me what you are planning. I appreciate that your intentions towards me and my family are well-meaning and charitable, but if I knew all of your plans, then perhaps I would be better able to show the proper gratitude."

"Cousin, you have suffered much in these past few months, while I stood by, powerless to alter the course of your family's fortunes. You may think I am acting out of charity, but it is actually family loyalty that pushes me to act. You are half Keeling – we share the same blood from the same proud lineage. While it is true that your father was not as highly ranked as mine, he was a good man who behaved as a gentleman. He spared no expense when it suited him to be charitable."

"You wish to help me because my father was a good man?"

"Yes, but more than that. I believe it is the proper thing to do. Please do not confuse me with my father. He is a noble in his own right, but he is driven by ambition and duty. I do not blame him, but I am not the same manner of person."

"No, you most certainly are not," Catherine replied as they arrived at the entrance of Almack's.

Gazing out the window, she was overcome by anxiety. This club represented all that society was, and all that it afforded to the elite and wealthy. Was she risking being spurned? Did she want to accompany her cousin into a place where she knew in her bones that she did not belong?

"Cousin, you appear pale and apprehensive," Denton said.

"Denton, are you certain that you can afford to be seen with me?" she asked, as she stared at the fashionable people assembled at the entrance.

"Of course I can be seen in your presence. You may not believe me, but you look very elegant, if I may say so. In that dress, you will undoubtedly be amongst the comeliest of ladies in attendance this evening. It would be my honour to be seen with you, here or anywhere else."

"Thank you, Denton," she replied as he stepped out of the carriage, so that he could assist her in descending to the street. As they were admitted to the club, Catherine felt the gaze of all of society upon her. She felt scrutinised and admired by the most powerful men and women in the city – perhaps in all of the country. Yet, she did not think the stares and whispers were reserved for her alone.

Denton Keeling was a rather stylish, attractive and unmarried aristocrat. Some of the attention was because of his handsome countenance.

"Denton, what are we to do here amongst these people?"

"We shall play cards, if you would enjoy a game of chance and skill. If not, there is dancing, and of course tea is served ... but that is not the principal reason why I have brought you to Almack's."

"What is the reason?" she asked hesitantly, as he led her through the throngs of well-dressed and fashionable people.

"You shall soon see. Come, let us have a cup of tea."

"Very well, if you insist."

Denton led her into the tearoom, to a table that was reserved for his small party. A nod towards the serving staff led to tea and refreshments being provided.

But that was not all that arrived at the table. An attendant rushed in, almost immediately as they were settled. The man held a note on a silver tray, which was delivered to Mr Keeling. He took the note and read it with a smile.

"Denton, is it good news?" Catherine asked.

"It is for me – and for you, my dear. In a moment, we shall be meeting a gentleman – a gentleman whom I hope you will recall from Brigham Park. I have just received word that he has arrived and will join us for tea momentarily."

"Who might that be?" Catherine asked, sensing the answer that was about to come.

"The Duke of Rotherham. I recall that you and he formed a sincere acquaintance in the last days of the party."

Catherine gasped. She struggled to compose herself as she slowly set the cup of tea on the table.

The duke was at Almack's that night. She did not even have time to wonder how such a meeting was possible, before she saw the duke, striding confidently across the room. As he drew near, his eyes met hers. She expected that he would turn away, or that he would greet her cousin with a great deal of haste and then excuse himself, but he did neither of those things. He returned her gaze as she stared at him.

From the moment she first saw him, onwards she did not remember much about the evening. The duke's every smile and kind word, no matter how small and insignificant, reminded her deeply and achingly of the pain she had felt in his presence before, but there was also another emotion. She felt gratitude that her cousin had managed to arrange for her to see the duke once again, even for only one night.

Chapter 20

It was not customary for proper young women from good families to ride out, unaccompanied by a groom or a chaperone. For this reason, and knowing how Catherine enjoyed riding, her cousin, Denton, had already made good on his offer to be of assistance to the family by providing a servant who could act as a manservant and groomsman to the family. Catherine was grateful, as she wished to enjoy the few freedoms she could, before beginning her search for a position amongst the very people she had observed at Almack's. If she was to be a governess by the summer or the autumn, then she was determined to cherish her relative liberty by riding in the park in the afternoons, especially when she needed to think of matters that were threatening to consume her.

The events of the previous evening weighed upon her as she rode. It was one of the few pleasures she found in these troubling times. Once again, she had reason to thank the tenderness of heart of Mr Lionel, an elderly neighbour who had been acquainted with her departed father. It was this dear man's kindness that allowed for the upkeep of her horse in London, as he permitted the animal to be stabled amongst his own. She was grateful that her father had enjoyed such fine connections, as it afforded her the extraordinary joy that riding permitted her. Riding helped clear her mind and let her find comfort when none was available elsewhere.

Today she wanted to ponder the demeanour of the duke. His arrival at Almack's had been unexpected. She should have been furious with her cousin for arranging such a startling turn of events, but she could not. The shock was too great – and so was her optimism. The duke had not treated her with the same distance and ill-feelings as he had when they had parted ways at Brigham Park. In fact, he had been friendly towards her, however that was all there was to the matter – nothing more, nothing less. He was simply being cordial as he would to any one of his acquaintances.

After watching him walk away from her, seemingly with no concern for the enormous heartbreak he had caused her, Catherine made a decision that alarmed even her, but which was necessary for her sanity. She promised herself she would not beg or plead for his notice – not after his insults and the terrible injury he had done her at Brigham Park. She would not pursue him at another time, no matter how desperately her heart wished for just that.

Catherine received some looks from the few women who were riding in carriages at this early hour of the afternoon. It was not unusual to see riders in the park, but it was rare to find a lady riding with a groomsman, or even going about in the open barouche, as the afternoons were normally reserved for paying social calls and tea. It was simply unfashionable to be seen in Hyde Park so early when the more popular times of the day were still several hours away.

As she rode, Catherine was able to take in the beauty of the trees and the wide expanses of lawn. It was not nostalgia that fuelled her unhappiness during her ride that day. She had seen the duke. Whether she was prepared for the shock of seeing him or not, she was forced to relive all of the emotions she had felt upon their last meeting, even as she wondered if he would recall that she had worn the same blue dress.

She sighed, deciding that she would return home. A cup of tea might be a better and smarter panacea for what ailed her. She signalled to the groom that she intended to return and made her way along the path, towards the entrance of the park. A rider was approaching her.

Her heart began racing as she realised that she was looking at the man who had made sleep impossible, since she had seen him the previous night. The Duke of Rotherham rode as confidently as he did all things. It seemed as if he had been born to be an expert equestrian, as well as a powerful aristocrat. She raised her head high and attempted to mirror the confidence she saw in him.

He slowed and tipped his hat to her. "Miss Conolly, a lovely day for riding."

"Your Grace, so it is," she answered, hoping her haughty manner hid her nervousness at the sight of him.

"How did you enjoy the cards at Almack's?" It was a polite question, which indicated that he was not rushing away as she assumed he would, after exchanging a simple greeting. Still, regardless of how warmly he had treated her yesterday at Almack's, Catherine had not forgotten the way he had dismissed her in the autumn, and she decided to keep the conversation respectful, but brief.

"The cards were an interesting diversion," she answered politely.

"I agree, Miss Conolly. The company at Almack's was rather unexpected."

"It certainly was ... Well, I should be leaving now. Good day to you," she said as she gripped the reins and prepared to leave him to his riding.

"Miss Conolly, if I may accompany you for the remainder of your ride?"

"I am in no position to decline your request, Sir, however, I wouldn't want to impose and keep you from your ride in the park," she answered. "Still, I wonder at your arrival. Is it not an odd coincidence that we have met each other again today?"

"You never fail to impress me with your boldness and your candour. I shall answer your question in the same tenor. As you may recall, my valet is a capable man of many talents. Your habit of riding out at this time of the day is a habit, I daresay, which is spoken of by your servants and was just the piece of news I hoped to discover."

"You sent your valet to speak to my servants? Are my servants so disloyal?"

"They are loyal, I give you my word. They offered him no more than your schedule...."

"I fear your time was wasted. There is not much to be discovered in my schedule. Since the autumn, my family resides in London where we are not often occupied by a great number of invitations or visitors."

"I consider the time to have been well spent. I was afforded this opportunity to speak to you, without the hindrances of convention or social obligations," he replied, without offering any further explanation concerning the startling nature of the news he had disclosed so openly. His confession regarding his wish to speak to her alone, should have caused her some surprise, but at this moment, she was attempting to guess his intentions.

"I should be angered at the intrusion, but I admit I am intrigued that you have endeavoured to discover a time when you may best meet with me in private. Although the manner of it was not entirely honourable, I should not be surprised, considering your propensity for mysterious errands in the late hours."

His lips formed into a smile, "You thought me to be a highwayman. Do you still believe me to be?"

"Perhaps," she answered briefly, not wanting to dwell on any subjects that may lead her to relive the nights she had spent in his company at Brigham Park.

"Did your cousin, Mr Keeling, not tell you that the highwayman and his band of brigands were caught soon after our party dispersed? As you can see for yourself ... I have not been hanged for thievery."

"Do you remind me of my folly, to make me feel ridiculous?" she asked, the old anger that he sparked inside of her returning.

She had actually tried her best to forget her cousin's words. He had told her that, during the highwayman's capture, the man had shouted out "Wharton made me do it. He's the true leader!" Since then, malicious gossip had spread, saying her uncle had been part of the raids, hiding his face behind the robber's mask. The wagging tongues also said that when it had seemed inevitable that the gang would be caught, he had tricked one of his fellow brigands into leading the raids – all in order to escape the hangman's rope himself.

In the end, there had not been enough real evidence to prove her uncle's guilt. That his sons increasingly turned away from him after the event spoke volumes, however. The only person who continued to believe in his complete innocence was Catherine's mother, who considered her brother's involvement with "the horrid fiends", as she called them, "simply and utterly ridiculous". Whether her support came from an effort to minimise the unavoidable scandal or because she was actually convinced of her brother's innocence, Catherine would never know.

"I remind you of it," he said, "not to make you feel foolish, but to reassure you that despite my methods, which may seem underhanded, I am an honourable gentleman.

"An honourable gentleman who sends his valet to snoop? The same man who confesses to arranging to meet a young woman with only a groom for her chaperone?"

He ignored her concerns. "Which has led me to this moment with you in the park on this lovely afternoon. It is a pity we are not on my estate, where we might ride without restraint."

She wanted to ask him about their last meeting at Brigham Park, but she did not dare. If he was content to act as he once had – not the duke who saved her from the scoundrel, Churchill, but a polite version of the man she knew – then, she was not going to question him about the unpleasantness of that fateful night at the ball.

"Is it your practice to bribe servants so you may gain an audience?" she asked, surprising herself by her bravery.

"It is not often my habit but, as I said, I was hesitant about renewing the acquaintance."

He did not say why, but she could guess the reason. "You did not wish to leave your card, or announce to society that you were known to my mother and myself?"

"Miss Conolly, if that was true, then would I have been seen in your company at Almack's? Do not concern yourself with the reasons for what I do. A man in my position must take precautions."

He did not say what those precautions may be, but she had the distinct feeling that he was referring to her uncle's scheme, although he did not say so directly.

With a deft change of subject, he inquired whether she had been bothered by Mr Churchill since leaving her uncle's residence. She returned his question with one of her own, concerning Miss Church-ill, which caused him to throw his head back and laugh. The sound was rich and deep. At the end of their ride, he respectfully asked to call upon her. This time he promised he would deal with the matter correctly, by leaving his card.

Catherine did not say no.

Chapter 21

Early spring had warmed into a pleasant season, becoming as fragrant with flowers and greenery as any season in Catherine's memory. For the past two months, she had no longer been an outcast amongst her own kind. She surmised the change had three reasons: her friendship with Lady Frederica, the invitations issued by her cousin while he was in London on business, and the appearance of the duke's carriage in parts of London that had not seen a personage of his rank in its history. His calling card became a common sight at the plain, unremarkable house and was found atop the increasingly large number of calling cards on display for visitors to view.

To Catherine's delight, she saw her mother smile in contentment as more and more ladies paid calls and commented on the duke's card as it lay amongst their own. A duke who was paying calls at the home of a baronet was unthinkable, but true!

That spring it was not just Mrs Conolly who delighted in the invitations and the social calls of the duke. Catherine's brother was not overlooked, after he had been introduced to His Grace, and he became a frequent guest at the duke's dinner table while he was in London. For Catherine, the friendship that was burgeoning between the duke and herself was unexpected, but she was not prepared to question or discourage it.

Over those same two months, they had become – if not inseparable – then on the best of terms possible for a gentleman and lady
who were not engaged. Her brother and her mother (to her amazement) were welcome at the duke's house and had been fixtures in his
drawing room for weeks. Nothing was ever mentioned about Mrs
Conolly's bragging or Catherine's part in her uncle's scheme. The
matter of Mr Churchill, her late-night escapades, and his habit of
roaming about the countryside after dark, were also not discussed.
Instead, it seemed to Catherine as if they had renewed an amiable
connection, with a fervour she had not experienced before that season began.

The duke and she often went riding in the park, accompanied by a
suitable chaperone. They visited the theatre together, as it was a distraction both enjoyed, as were cards at Almack's. The entire season
passed in a whirlwind, and in a stream of joy and amity that Catherine dared not address for fear that if she brought up the past or
drew attention to her feelings, then the connection between the duke
and her would be severed. Sometimes she wondered what had
changed to make him suddenly treat her as a dear friend. Why had
he never asked about Brigham Park – not even once? It had come as
a surprise to her that he was suddenly no longer reluctant to
acknowledge their connection. As a matter of fact, his invitations to
dine were as frequent as his appearances at tea or riding alongside
her in the park.

By not addressing or acknowledging what nearly everyone else in
London seemed to presume '*the Duke of the Moors and the daughter of a penniless baronet*' were fast becoming one of the most discussed couples of the season.

Catherine was afraid that rumours were being spoken in every fashionable drawing room in Mayfair and she was right.

However, by not addressing what everyone assumed was a match, she grew terribly despondent and worried about it. Catherine felt she could no longer avoid her feelings for him, which had grown with every passing day, and his avoidance of speaking about his regard for her or his intentions, worried her. The season drew closer to its end with every passing day, and she wondered what would happen when he returned to his estate at Halton Heath and she was left in town. She wondered how she would recover after two blissful months of dancing with him, and of laughing as they rode in the park, or played cards together. How was she to return to her dull and uneventful life once he tired of her companionship?

So it was, with great determination and considerable trepidation, that she chose to take a risk she feared would have consequences that she could not bear. Her future as a governess, or someone else's future prospect, depended on whether the duke had any intentions towards her at all, especially since Catherine had a secret that she shielded and guarded as carefully as a prized possession. She dared not confess the depth of her regard for him, but she could not escape it, either. She was desperately and madly in love with him!

On a rainy afternoon, which did not permit their customary ride in the park, His Grace arrived at the door of her modest residence. The drawing room was not full, but it held a respectable number of ladies who had come to call upon Catherine's mother. Many of those ladies were of a *certain class* that was not amongst the peers known to the Duke of Rotherham. While it was not proper amongst society to be alone in the presence of a gentleman, Catherine invited him into their small, austere sitting room. The door was left open, and the footman stood outside the open door, at a slight distance. The room had a thin wall, and the cheerful sounds of the ladies' conversation could be heard in a muted manner. The duke was not a complete stranger, nor was he a new acquaintance. The closeness of her connection to him, and his amiable friendship with her brother, but mostly her wish to talk to him privately, prompted Catherine to seize the opportunity. She asked the duke to be seated in one of a pair of upholstered chairs in the room. A cane settee was positioned by the fireside, a writing desk at the window, and a threadbare rug covered the floor. Catherine knew that she should be embarrassed to invite a duke into a room not fit for the servants' hall in Brigham Park, but the room was neat and clean. Despite its plainness, the room afforded them a modicum of privacy, which was what she required for the conversation that lay ahead.

"Shall I ring for tea?" she asked him, aware of his handsome features and his sparkling grey eyes, as she willed herself not to engage in long gazes in his direction.

"Perhaps later. I regret we shall not be able to go for our afternoon ride. It is one of the things I shall miss about town when I return home to my estate in a fortnight."

She felt his words pierce her chest, as if physically. Whispering, she asked, "You are leaving in a fortnight? Has the season come to an end so swiftly?"

"It has, I am afraid. I have been away longer than I would have liked. I am not often away from my estate for such a prolonged period of time." He offered her a smile.

Did he mean anything by that smile, she wondered as she studied him and his gaze with a scrutiny that she prayed he would not find intrusive.

"I presumed you would remain until summer."

"Summer is nearly upon us. Have you not observed the changes that we see in the park's verdure?"

She had, but she had been quick to deny them. Looking down as the modest laughter and lilting voices of the women, exchanging gossip and advice wafted through the walls, permitted a distraction from the tumultuous emotions she was experiencing. Did she dare to ask her question? Did she dare say what was in her heart?

"This may not be an opportune time to ask," she began, her voice sounding unsure and wobbly, "but I do not know if we will have many other moments to speak without being overheard by others. There is a question that has weighed upon my mind for some time, although I have not dared to ask it until now."

"Miss Conolly, there is no question that you may pose that will offend or offer me insult."

"It is about Brigham Park. We never discuss it. Why have we never addressed what happened?" she asked, her eyes searching his for answers, as she gained some strength from confronting the worst fears of her heart.

"Your capacity for forgiveness has astonished me," he replied in a quiet, serious manner.

"Forgiveness?" she asked.

"Many things have happened since that fateful night at the ball. Your uncle's upturn in his fortunes, thanks to his son's keen head for business ... your own drop in circumstances. I do not want to insult you, but you and I have always spoken honestly."

"Yes, we have," she said.

"As you are aware, in Yorkshire, rivalries amongst noble families are deep and treacherous. I will not deceive you, I have long wanted Brigham Park for my own. Not because my estate is lacking, but because I wished to possess the property to ruin your uncle. However, once he becomes viscount, your cousin will not be a rival to me, but instead an acquaintance who I consider worthy of my friendship. It is strange to think that I respect your cousin ... whereas your uncle, I am afraid, is another matter entirely."

"You once accused me of being my uncle's pawn."

"I did, and I recall that conversation with regret. I learned that with your change in fortune, you were not a willing participant in your uncle's schemes. Your cousin, Mr Keeling, has been very forthcoming regarding that matter. He has stood up for your character at the expense of his own father's reputation.

"A matter which I have not revealed. I shall not ruin the man's name despite his plans to entrap me, not for the sake of Mr Keeling, but for you. It has been made known to me that you did not have the slightest intention to secure a match with me in order to further your uncle's position, or your own. I understand a marriage of convenience could easily have been made, such as with the Earl of Burwickshire, who would marry you without hesitation."

"He is a generous and kind man. I am honoured to call His Lordship and his sister my friends."

"Precisely. You have not taken advantage of them or anyone else. You have allowed yourself to sink to your current level rather than snare some other soul, to save yourself or your family from ruin. That may sound like an insult or a terrible reference, but to me, it is evidence of a strength of character."

Her brow furrowed. She was attempting to understand his words. "Is that the reason you have resumed your acquaintance with me and the reason that you have offered me your friendship?"

"Yes, Miss Conolly. I am offering you my friendship, my highest regard and my esteem."

She bowed her head signalling her gratitude to him. The question of what the future held in store hung in the air between them but remained unspoken.

That is, until, he said, "This season is ending, I must return to my estate. I have been away for far too long."

"I understand," she answered quietly.

She did understand.

It was the end of the season, and the two months she had spent falling in love with him were coming to an end. At that moment, she realised that there could be no future for her and a duke. The distance between them in terms of rank and property were simply too vast. Catherine contented herself with the knowledge that the duke had risked his own reputation to befriend her and her family publicly and had effectively helped to regain some of their status in society. Something had been left unsaid. When their eyes met, a spark seemed to be present for an instant. She was not certain, but for a moment, in the quietness of their London sitting room, she felt a connection to him that was deeper than any she could have imagined.

It was unfortunate that in a fortnight, he would be gone to his grand house in Yorkshire and she would be left in London, with a broken heart.

Chapter 22

Summer in Yorkshire was filled with a beauty that was desolate but breath-taking. As the carriage rumbled over the hills, Catherine gazed out at the scenery, reflecting on when she had first visited this lonely place. Her mother sat across from her, just as she had that terrible night they had been attacked by highwaymen on this same road. Now, the endless stretch of wild land was covered in a bright pink and mauve carpet of heather which bloomed for mile after mile. Its beauty was far from the sombre sight the moors had been when Catherine had first travelled the road – when a threat had lurked with a menace that felt palpable. That threat had vanished. The highwayman – no matter his true identity – and his band of thieves were gone. In their place Catherine imagined that peace returned to the moorland.

She read the invitation she held in her hand, once again. Although there would be no attack this time, Catherine realised that she still felt a measure of apprehension. This time, it was caused by the paper that she was holding. The invitation was from the duke and was extended to her family. He had invited them to his estate, *Crawborne Castle* at Halton Heath in Yorkshire. Catherine's brother promised to join them as soon as he was free of his responsibilities in town. Jane remained in London with Patience, and so Catherine and her mother were travelling from London to Yorkshire alone.

It was a long journey, and it gave Catherine time to wonder about what had prompted the duke's invitation.

Of course, her mother was certain that a proposal of marriage would follow. "Oh, child. My goodness, you will be a duchess soon! See, I have been right all along."

But none of that had been mentioned in London, or even a hint of such a promise. Catherine knew the duke. If he invited her brother as well as her, then he was being generous and kind. Catherine knew he was not asking for her hand, even though her heart wished for nothing more.

The carriage arrived at the great house without incident. The home, an enormous and foreboding edifice, four-stories high, was designed in the manner of many of the northern houses. It was built as a citadel against attack by marauding Scottish hoards. The grey stone of its façade was punctuated by turrets and towers of every manner of battlement. It reminded her of Brigham Park, but it was clearly larger and far more imposing.

From the castle, one only had to go a little bit further to find the moors, and with them, a mysterious world of legends. Catherine gasped at the incredible wealth and power that was conveyed by the residence, which was the seat of the Dukedom of Rotherham, and promised herself she would try not to be anxious when she was with His Grace. It was a promise she would most likely fail to keep.

He received them warmly and saw to their comfort immediately. He welcomed them to his vast home, a house that was a testament to strength and unimaginable prestige. Once she was in these sur-roundings, Catherine understood why he was arrogant, the manner with which he carried himself and much else about him. He commanded the respect of his peers by being distantly related to a long line of the royal family. The conceit and arrogance that had long been his most obvious trait to her (aside from his extremely handsome features) no longer hindered their renewed connection.

Often, they rode along the hillsides of the moors, galloping as fast as they wished. When they were letting the horses run, they rode together at a peaceful pace.

It was during such tranquil moments, that she discovered, quite by accident, that she had come to adore this landscape that had once filled her with fear.

She was entranced by the beauty of the moors. The changes in the landscape, from a dreary lifeless place to a vibrant heath, were astonishing. She no longer saw the moors as lands of danger and cold relentless winds, which chilled her. As she rode at the side of the duke, she realised the moor was a place of ethereal beauty. The hills were transformed into a lush rolling landscape, resplendent in shades of green. The rocks were not foreboding gravestones, but were monuments, ancient sentinels that dotted the landscape magisterially. There was a unique loveliness in the flowers of the moors, which bloomed in colours that were brilliant and surprising. In the company of the duke, she found the land to be so riveting that she could scarcely take her eyes from the vivid scenery. Somehow, she had fallen in love with the rugged beauty of the North Country. It was odd, she mused, how she had ever seen this land in any other way.

When they were not riding together on the moors, they spent afternoons perusing his collection of books, talking freely about the works. They enjoyed tea together, as her mother embroidered quietly and contently nearby. The visit to Crawborne Castle was totally delightful, and yet it seemed to Catherine, that once again, he had not mentioned a word about the future, neither hers, nor his own. He behaved as a most attentive suitor, but nothing was said to indicate that he considered himself to be courting her.

As one week became another, her brother Henry joined them. Catherine's mother assured her that the duke had been waiting for this moment, and they would surely soon be party to an exciting announcement. However, when her brother left for London without any announcement being made, she began to despair of the duke's feeling as she did. Was she in love with him, whereas he regarded her as merely a dear companion – someone who eased his boredom?

He treated her as grandly as she presumed any man in love may, but he did not speak those words to her. *Their friendship seemed to be enough to satisfy him*, or so she thought, which was leading her into a dilemma that she could no longer avoid. What was to be done about her future? Being friends with the duke meant that he could supply her with a reference, but no prospects would come from the friendship. She was neither married, nor seeking a position during the time she spent as his friend. While she dreaded to consider what she had to do, her family was not in a position to afford her this life of tea, riding, and dining. Her family's debts were considerable, and her family was desperate for money.

Catherine knew the time had come, as she strolled along a path in the gardens of Crawborne Castle one sunny afternoon in July. She had to find a position as governess soon. She had no wish to continue being a burden on her poor brother, Henry.

High overhead a bird chirped happily in the warm sunlight. She mused that she may take a flower to press in a book as a memory of her time here, and as a memento of her friendship with a man she had come to love and respect. How different were her feelings for him to the time when she had thought he was the leader of the highwaymen. Back then, she was passionate about him, trapped in feelings of temptation and aghast at his arrogance. As she selected a wildflower from a bush, covered in tender violet blooms, she realised that her feelings for him had altered. They were gentle now, softer somehow, but no less powerful.

"Miss Conolly, there you are. I have been searching for you," the duke said as he approached her.

"I did not see you there, Your Grace. I hope you do not mind that I plucked a few flowers."

"No," he replied, but he seemed slightly distracted. "You may pick as many as you wish."

"These will do. I have taken them as mementoes. I want to remember this place, this summer and," she hesitated to say it, but then she plunged forward, "... you."

"You picked these flowers to remember me?"

"I have. Was my confession too forward?" she asked breathlessly.

"Your confession is not forward, not among us. I wonder, Miss Conolly, if you would do me the honour of taking a walk with me?"

"I can think of nothing I would rather do than walk with you."

They walked beside one another for a few minutes, before Catherine addressed him. "There is something I wish to say to you," she said as she looked at him, and then turned away.

"You may tell me anything that is in your heart, but first, would you indulge me? I have something I want to tell you ... something that I pray will not alter your opinion of me."

"Nothing you say could alter my opinion of you. I spoke to you even when I thought you were a common thief. Do you recall?" she said with a smile.

"How well I recall. Which is how I know that you are capable of independent thought, which has not been the mark of many others around me. It is because of your free manner of thinking – and at times speaking – that I value you as a dear friend. It is the reason I must share news with you that may alter our acquaintance."

She felt the pain in her chest at his words. She had long suspected that he would have to find a wife amongst his own rank, someone whose family was as wealthy and privileged as his own, but she was not prepared for that news to come now. Had that been the real reason for the invitation to his house?

She spoke bravely, "If you wish to tell me that you have found a wife ... or wish me gone from your life, I understand. I pray that you will say it quickly so that it may lessen the pain. I knew this friendship between us was no more than a mere few months of amusement to you. I have cherished it, knowing that it could not last. I pray you will have every happiness."

He stopped walking and turned to look at her, surprised. "Miss Conolly, you are mistaken. I have no wish to say goodbye just yet, but *you* might ... when you learn of what I have to tell you."

"Oh, what is it?"

"Please listen, and then you may decide what is to be done."

"I will listen," she said as confidently as she was able to.

"Miss Conolly, it is a tale that I will only share with you, because I have come to care for you. I am indebted to you. You have changed my life."

"I have?" she asked quietly.

"Yes, you have. You may recall that terrible night at Brigham Park when I spoke so rudely ... I was speaking from experience, but you could not know that. My story begins when I was a young man. I was the second son. I was never meant to become the duke. That honour fell to my older brother."

She gasped.

"Yes, Miss Conolly. I had a brother – just one, Robert. My mother died after I was born. For many years, he was the heir and I was a man seeking to make my way in the world. I was young and filled with ideals ... I was not the cynical man you beheld at Brigham Park."

"What happened to change you into a cynical sort of man?"

"I will tell you. Perhaps then you will understand why I have treated you appallingly ... and why I have applauded your capacity to forgive me when I did not deserve it. Miss Conolly, you have shown me how wrong I was to judge all people, and for that, I thank you."

"I forgave you a long time ago, because of my regard for you. Not many men in your position would have acknowledged a connection to a woman of my rank."

"Not many women would have forgiven me for my harsh words and my cruelty to you. It is for that reason that I owe you the truth."

"You do not owe me a debt of any kind. If you never revealed the reason for your actions, I would be content to know you as you are," she assured him.

"That would not be enough, not now. If you will hear me out."

She nodded her head, and he began a story she did not expect. He spoke as he had, a moment before telling her of his father's plans for his brother and his own plans, which would have led him to a life as an officer in the army – a life that was not to be.

"I was ready to become an officer. My father promised me the necessary money for my commission, and I was certain that I would become a colonel, so I devoted my time to that end." He paused and looked into her eyes. "There was a woman."

Catherine was not anticipating feeling envy for a woman, of whom he spoke in the past tense, but she did. Quietly, she dismissed those feelings of jealousy and urged him to continue.

"I loved her with all the passion of a young man in the throes of his first love. I did not know, but she had designs on my brother. When I spoke to her of my love, and asked her to be my bride, she agreed. We were happy! I promised her that she would become the wife of an officer and that I would do anything to make her happy. I introduced her to my family.

Soon after, she told me, without any care for my pain, that as I was the second son and not going to inherit the estate or the title, she could not marry a man without property. She broke my heart and ruined any aspirations I had for love. I am ashamed to admit that she did more than break my heart. She declared her interest in my brother simply because of his money and title. That declaration turned me away from love, forever."

"What happened? Did she marry your brother?" Catherine wondered, as she sympathised with the pain he had endured.

He shook his head. "She did not marry him, or anyone else. My father died before I joined the army, leaving my brother to become the duke. I stayed on to assist him and to settle our father's affairs. He did not marry that woman or any other. He died of a sudden illness within a few months of my father's death, leaving me alone in the world. I quickly found myself the Duke of Rotherham. I should caution you – at this point the story takes a turn that I fear you will not wish to hear."

"Whatever turn it may take, I want to hear of it."

With a deep breath, he exhaled and then said, "There was a child born out of wedlock."

She gasped and then immediately regained her composure. "I am sorry. Was the child... is the child yours?"

He shook his head. "The child, a little girl, is the daughter of my brother. The woman of whom I spoke of earlier, was determined to win my brother at any price. When he died unexpectedly, she was left unwed and soon to become a mother."

"Oh, and what became of the little girl?"

"When we first met, you asked me about my mysterious errands at Brigham Park ... errands I kept secret because I felt that I had to. Can you guess why I was absent from the hunting party?" he asked.

"I think I know, but please continue..."

"I shall tell you. The errands were to see the child. For many years I searched for her, not knowing what had become of her. She was missing for most of her life, as the woman who was her mother was disgraced. She returned to her native North Country and established herself in a situation as a laundress and sewing woman. She became ill there and, sadly, she perished in the last days of the past summer. The child, now a pitiable orphan, has been in the care of a kind family who cannot afford to keep her, as they have many children of their own. I discovered that the child was recently found in a village near Brigham Park, after I arrived in the autumn."

Catherine found herself recalling the rumours about him, the lost love, the mysterious woman who disappeared upon the moors as she said, "Then it is true, the rumours about you and the woman you loved. Your love was lost, she vanished."

"You have heard the idle gossip that surrounds me," he answered. "I am not astonished. The circumstances of the woman's sudden departure have been the cause of much speculation. She is said to have died upon the moors, of heartbreak or some other nonsense. People will talk, will they not?"

"You were going to see this child? What is her name?" Catherine asked, shifting back to the more relevant and real possibility of what he was trying to confess to her, about the child and her mother. Her own heart ached to think of a young baby, made an orphan on the woeful demise of her mother. Yet even as she longed to know of the little girl, she was fearful. She was afraid that at the end of the story, he would tell her that he was still in love with the woman who had once broken his heart and given birth to his niece. That his love for her, although she was departed, had not ceased, and he was not free of the heartbreak she had caused with her ambition.

"Yes, Miss Conolly. The girl is my niece. She is young – five years this May. Her mother named her Louisa. Due to the circumstances of her birth, I was ashamed to acknowledge her, but I still wished to help her in this world. I did not intend to abandon her, even if I could not publicly acknowledge her, nor was I certain I wished to. Her mother ruined me. She destroyed any chance I had of finding happiness with anyone after her."

"Are ... you still in love with her?" Catherine willed herself to breathe after saying that out loud.

The duke stopped walking.

He turned to her and reached for her hands.

"I am not in love with her any longer. I have not been in love with her for a very long time. I am ashamed that I did not tell you about my niece before now, but I was not sure that I ever could forgive her mother for breaking my heart. Miss Conolly ... Catherine, it is be-cause of you – because of your warm and patiently loving company that I have learned how to trust and love again. Because of you, I have changed my way of thinking about my past and the woman I once thought I loved. I have forgiven her, even though that for-giveness has come too late to ease the hardships of her life. I was unable to reconcile with her while she was alive ... but I have made a decision that I pray you will understand."

Catherine followed his story in silence, and she knew what he was going to say.

Confidently, he stated, "I have decided to claim the little girl as my niece, publicly, and without reservation. I wish for the child to be raised in my household, and to have the finest governesses and tutors that my money can buy."

Following his confession, Catherine was reeling from all that he had revealed.

"Please say something. I have bared my soul to you," the duke urged her, as he stared into her eyes.

"Sir," she began, "I am astonished by your story."

"I was afraid that you might be. If you have no wish to continue our friendship, tell me now, and I shall never bother you again."

She sighed as she replied, "Oh, but I have every wish to continue our friendship! I thought I knew who you were, but I was wrong. I respect you even more for forgiving that poor young woman, but more so for wanting to acknowledge your niece, even if she was born out of wedlock."

He smiled at her with the warmest smile she had ever seen on his face.

"There is something I have known for a long time," Catherine continued. "It is something I have treasured and that I want to tell you now." She closed her eyes. She willed herself to open them again as she confessed what was in her heart. "I am in love with you. I was in love with you before this moment, but your kindness to your niece and your forgiveness of the woman who caused you pain, has made my feelings for you even stronger than they were."

"You love me?" he asked.

"I do. But I do not expect for you to return my feelings. How can you? You must marry a woman who is accomplished, a person who is deserving of the title of duchess and who may further your connections and increase your wealth. It has been my honour to know you and to know that you are a man worthy of my admiration. I will always pray for your happiness."

"You would wish me to marry a woman, to be happy, even as you admit to loving me?"

"Yes, I would wish you anything that assures your happiness."

"Catherine, would *you* consent to marrying me?"

Catherine stood in shock. "You cannot mean that," she said as she peered into his grey eyes, searching for the truth behind his words.

"I do not care for money or titles. I have both and do not need either. You have proven to me, though you did not set out to do so, that you are capable of love without avarice. You wish for my happiness, even at the expense of your own. You have shown me that love is real and true. You have given me a reason to love again. Oh, how I fought against that feeling! I tried to keep you at a distance, but I failed. You won me a long time ago, although you did not know it."

There on the garden path, he took her hand in his and repeated his words, "I ask again. Will you marry me, my dearest Catherine? Will you become my duchess?"

Tears of happiness fell down her face and it seemed the birds were singing just for them.

"Yes, I will."

At her 'yes' he gazed at her and his grey eyes promised love and devotion forever. He took her into his strong arms, pulling her close, and kissed her. It was a kiss as sweet and tender as her love for him had become. On that day, she did not think that she could love him anymore than she did. In the years to come, she would discover, quite pleasantly, that she was wrong.

She would love him more every day of all the years of their long life together as man and wife – as the Duke and Duchess of the Moors.

Dear Reader,

Did you enjoy my romance novel? Then you might enjoy other Regency novels in the Wharton series:

An Orphan for the Duke

Seven years ago, the Duke of Devonshire's heart was shattered. After his late-wife's death, the duke immersed himself in work and duty so he could numb the pain. Despite his possession of immense wealth, a historic title, strikingly handsome looks, and not few possible prospects, he wants for nothing in this world – except to be left alone.

That solitude ends suddenly with the arrival of a desperate letter from an old friend, containing his dying wish that the duke care for his daughter. The duke, unable to ignore his dying friend's appeal, orders the house to be prepared for the child's arrival – much-loved toys and dolls, a room with the best views in the front of the house, and a swing in the garden. Only a few days later, Isabella arrives at the luxurious Hardwick Manor. She is a shock to the duke – in both age and appearance. He was expecting a child, and not a stunningly beautiful woman!

A Bride for the Viscount's Cold Son

After the premature death of her mother, young Lavinia is left destitute, with no money and no family. Until... in a twist of fate, she discovers her wealthy grandmother. Her new world of privilege doesn't just bring expensive gowns and jewels, but also a chance for love. The breathtakingly handsome son of the Viscount of Wharton has dazzling green eyes – but a conceit so profound that Lavinia isn't sure if he could possibly be the romantic hero she has been dreaming of...

Find a short reading sample of both books on the next pages.

Would you like to be informed as soon as the next volume in the series is published?

If so, I'd love to invite you to sign up to my mailing list: www.audreyashwood.com/releases
I will send you a short message via email as soon as the next books are ready to go. Subscribers will receive a chance to read them for free.

Yours,

Audrey Ashwood

Sneak Peek – An Orphan for the Duke

Coming 2020!

A broken duke.

An unexpected arrival.

Can her presence heal the man who swore never to love again?

Matthew Danvers, the Duke of Devonshire, buried his hopes with his beloved wife. So although he accepts a childhood friend's dying wish and takes guardianship of his daughter, a joyless manor is no place to raise a young child. But when the orphaned girl steps out of her carriage, he is stunned to discover she is actually a beautiful woman.

Isabella Thornton is alone in the world. Though the imposing duke has graciously taken her in, his cold, distant manner tells her she should better not overstay her welcome. Resolved to wed the first suitor who will have her, she struggles to reject her budding feelings for her strikingly handsome host.

With each moment spent with his charge, Matthew feels the ice melting around his heart. But with courting season approaching and a secret from Isabella's past threatening her prospects, he fears he will fail in his obligation as a ward. And even if he could help her, he cannot deny she may be everything he needs.

Can a heavy-hearted duke and a sunny young woman find their way to a future of love?

An Orphan for the Duke is a standalone, sweet Regency romance. If you like charming love stories, honourable heroes, and lush period settings, then you'll adore Audrey Ashwood's touching tale.

Read *An Orphan for the Duke* to experience unexpected passion today!

Reading Sample:

"Miss Isabella Thornton and company have arrived, Your Grace."

"At such a late hour?" the duke wondered.

"I shall greet them in the parlour."

The footman bowed his head and left.

After several weeks of anticipating this event, Isabella had arrived at Hardwick Manor, at last. *How unfortunate that his mother and sister were not in residence to greet the child*, he thought. The two were not due to return from London until the following day, leaving him burdened with the responsibility of seeing to the child. Still, he would take it upon himself to greet the guests and determine if the girl was well. If she was fit, then his housekeeper, Mrs Claxton, could manage without him. His book and his brandy would not have to wait long, he presumed. He did not plan to tarry in the new guests' company for too long.

Dispatching the butler with a few orders, the duke told the man what must be done. "See to their bags and trunks. Send for

Mrs Claxton. If she is not awake, see that she is awakened at once, I have need of her."

With his footman and butler sent about their tasks, the duke prepared himself to greet his guests. That the child was John's daughter should have been a reason for him to pause, but he was incapable of feeling any emotion other than worry. Why had the child arrived in such an untimely manner? Why could she not have arrived when his mother was in residence to attend to her?

He left the library and walked along the corridor leading to the hall.

He entered the parlour.

The silence that greeted him was not what he was expecting. He did not see anyone or hear any sound that may indicate he had a youthful visitor. He did observe that the drawing room door was ajar, however. *Would his footman have left a small child and company in the drawing room, a room filled with priceless objects such as the figurines and gilded statues that his mother adored*, he thought, worried about the child breaking something. As he approached the door, he hesitated. This was John's daughter; he did not wish to appear an old, ill-tempered man to a young girl – that would never do. Even he could see that. Willing himself to appear less imposing, he was buoyed by the fact that Mrs Claxton would arrive soon, to trundle the little girl off to the nursery. The housekeeper might give her a bowl of stew or some other suitable evening meal. He smiled and willed himself to appear as benevolent and kind as he could manage before, finally, entering the room.

He was astonished by the sight before him.

Inside the drawing room, a woman stood at the opposite end by the wall of windows.

Moonlight flooded through the panes of glass, bathing her features in a soft glow. Her pale skin was illuminated by the soft light, and her brown hair glistened as all around the moonlight danced and played, making her appear like an angel, despite her being dressed in the dark garb of mourning. She must not have heard him approach because she did not turn to face him. She remained with her face lifted towards the light.

He stood, motionless, appreciating the statuesque figure of the beauty who slowly opened her eyes, as if she was enraptured by the view of the full moon on the lawn that lay just beyond the window. As he observed her, watching for any indication that she was a ghostly form or the result of his imagination, he dared not speak. He was awestruck by her, as he would be of a magnificent view of a painting.

Matthew was accustomed to being in complete control of all that he felt and all that he surveyed. Yet, at this moment, as he stared at the beautiful woman, who stood unaware of his observation, he was lost for words. However, it was but only for a moment. He quickly quelled the emotion he felt welling within. He dismissed his own reaction to her as astonishment, at having a visitor so late in the evening and nothing more. He was a duke, for heaven's sake, he was not a boy, besot by beauty. He was not in the habit of feeling awed for *any* reason. He was not one to stand in stupefaction gazing at the beauty in front of him. It was time to address her.

"My footman informed me that I have a visitor. Whom am I addressing?" he asked formally. "Have you arrived with the child?"

She turned to face him – her deep-blue eyes were as pleasant as the graceful features of her oval face. *Who was this young woman – the child's nurse or her governess, perhaps?* He wondered, even though her wardrobe did not announce her to be either of those.

She lowered her head and curtsied. "It is a pleasure to make your acquaintance, Your Grace. I am Isabella Thornton, the daughter of the Earl of Chatham."

He stood silent, trying to make sense of her words.

"I have travelled with my maid. I believe she is seeing to the matter of my trunks," she continued, her voice as delightful as music played gently on a harp.

"*You* are Miss Isabella Thornton?" he asked as he tried to reconcile the woman who was standing in front of him with the image of a young child.

"I am known as Miss Thornton, Sir." She smiled. "I was told that you were expecting me."

...

End of the Reading Sample.

An Orphan for the Duke will be available on Amazon in 2020.

Sneak Peek – A Bride for the Viscount's Cold Son

A Traditional Historical Romance by Audrey Ashwood

A poor village orphan.
An unexpected fortune.
Can she overcome her humble beginnings to find true love?

Regency London. Lavinia Talridge is heartbroken. Struggling to survive after her mother's death, she discovers a wealthy grandmother and a second chance. Before she can believe her new life is true, Lavinia has an arranged marriage to a handsome gentleman and a chance at love.

But when the Viscount's son acts coldly towards her, Lavinia assumes her lower-class background is to blame. Afraid to go through with the potentially joyless marriage, can the former villager find a lifetime worth of love?

A Bride for the Viscount's Cold Son is a sweet Regency romance with a dash of suspense. If you like authentic women, tender moments, and changing fortunes, then you'll love Audrey Ashwood's delightful story.

Reading Sample:

The vicar invited Lavinia to stay at the rectory for a few days, but she declined his offer. Instead, she left with a hamper of food from the vicar's kitchen and a few pennies in her pocket.

The village had always been her home and when she walked along the narrow lanes of Cotes Cross, she realized that she knew every building and every house that crowded the streets. The buildings were old, like the village, and built of grey stone and timber. Today, she felt old too, far older than her years. She also felt alone.

Lavinia could have accepted the kindness of the vicar and the thatcher's or the other friendly villagers who kept inquiring about her well-being, but how could she be a burden to any of these people who had barely enough for themselves? She needed time to sort out the thoughts that were swirling in her head. Her chest hurt from the grief, her face was wet from crying, and her feet and hands were stinging from the cold. She saw the sympathetic looks of the people she passed on the street, as she made her way home to the cottage. Everyone in this small hamlet knew everyone else, and there were no secrets in Cotes Cross. Lavinia could feel the pity emanating from her well-meaning neighbours. One day soon, she might need to rely on that pity to live. Today, she needed to be at home, in the one place that reminded her of her mother.

Opening the wooden door of the cottage, she heard the familiar creak of the hinges. It used to be a welcoming sound when neighbours came to call, bringing their sewing to her mother. For a moment, the creaking hinges brought a smile to her face as she recalled happier times. Then she closed the door behind her and stood alone in the room. The cottage was cold, and the thick walls held the chill of winter. She set the hamper down on the rough-hewn table and gazed at the place on the floor where her mother had died.

The pallet was gone and with it all traces of the tragedy that had stolen her mother away from her. The hearth was swept, and a stack of fresh firewood lay in the fireplace. She did not know who had arranged the funeral, or who had paid for the coffin, but she could feel the generosity of her neighbours. In this tiny village in Yorkshire, her mother's friends were generous to her even in death. This was a moment that would live with Lavinia for a long time.

Sitting beside her own fireside, she noticed her mother's sewing box on the table beside the hamper of food, and a pile of mending sat neatly folded beside it. Lavinia wiped her tears from her eyes and wondered if she might find enough work mending and sewing just as her mother had done. She was strong for her age, despite her tiny frame. She could work; she could do odd jobs to earn money.

Would anyone pay her to do their sewing and mending? She crossed the tiny room and picked up a shirt, holding it up and looking at it. The tiny even stitches were nearly invisible, evidence of her mother's skill with a needle. She thought of what the vicar had said about her mother's talent and questioned whether she could do the same.

Her own sewing skills were coming along, as her mother used to say. She would allow Lavinia to help make mattress ticking or pillow cases, but that was all. Lavinia was not allowed to sew clothes, at least not yet. Her mother had dreams for Lavinia – dreams that she said would come true one day. Her mother prayed that Lavinia would not be a plain-sewing woman; she was not going to do odd jobs around the village to buy food. She was going to be married, perhaps to a tradesman or a farmer?

How Lavinia wished she shared her mother's hopes... She folded the shirt and placed it back on the pile. What could a girl of her age do in the world? She and her mother had lived plainly. The cottage and its sparse furnishings were all she had ever known, but she knew that other people did not live the way she had. The vicar, for example, and his wife had a nice house; their sitting room contained two upholstered chairs and a set of polished candlesticks. Maybe she could find work in a kitchen at a great house?

She thought about working in a manor house, cleaning and polishing all day long. The work would be hard, but she would have plenty of food to eat and a bed of her own. But would she want to leave the only place she had ever known? This cottage with these two tiny rooms had been her home since she was a child. Her neighbours had been the only people, aside from her Mama, whom she knew. Their children were her friends and the women were like aunts to her. She had not lied to the vicar when he asked her about her family, but she felt a twinge of guilt. She *did* have a family, but they were not related by blood – they were the people of Cotes Cross. If she left the village, she wouldn't know anyone, and no-one would know her. Lavinia had always been a quiet, timid child and the prospect of striking out for herself was nearly as frightening as starving in the streets.

The tears came again as she stared into the fire. The vicar had said to have faith. She had faith, but she did not know if faith was enough to save her.

A loud rapping at the door startled Lavinia so terribly that she jumped. Was it the landlord coming for the rent? *I should have stayed at the vicar's,* she thought, as she sat still, too panicked to move. She could pretend she was not home, but the smoke coming out of the chimney told a different story. Maybe she could give him all the money she had and promise to pay the rest in a week or two? Trembling in fear, Lavinia opened the narrow wooden box on the mantle and removed the meagre amount of coins, counting them.

It was not enough.

With her coins gripped tightly in her hand, she walked to the door, praying that God would have mercy on her. Lavinia opened the door and then immediately stepped back, gasping.

A man stood at the door. He was a tall man dressed in a black coat. She had never seen him before.

"Good day, is this the residence of Miss Lavinia Dean?" he asked as he tipped his hat.

Lavinia had never been called 'Miss' before and she had never had a man tip his hat to her. She did not know what to make of his strange behaviour. Peering past his hulking frame she saw a sight that was even more astonishing. A carriage was parked on the road, a few steps behind the man. The carriage was unlike any she had ever seen. It had a team of four milk-coloured horses and a gilt crest on the door. It looked like the type of carriage that belonged to lords and ladies, when they rode through town.

Lavinia did not know what the carriage or this man was doing at her cottage, but she tried to remember her manners. "I am Lavinia. I do not have much to offer you, but a seat at my fire."

"That is very kind of you, young Miss. I am the coachman. My mistress wishes to see you."

To Lavinia's astonishment, she watched transfixed as the coachman strode to the carriage. He opened the door and then stood straight and tall, as a woman emerged. Like Lavinia, she was short in stature and thin, but that was where the resemblance ended. The woman who stepped down from the carriage was richly attired in a fur-lined coat and a matching bonnet. She was an older woman, but she was handsome. She smiled at Lavinia.

"Lavinia? Can it be?"

Lavinia did not know this woman who reached out for her. With a curtsey, she answered, "Ma'am, won't you come inside?"

"Thank you, but I won't be staying long... and neither will *you*," the woman said as she bustled past Lavinia and headed inside to the fire.

Against the backdrop of the plaster walls, the dirt floor, and the rough wooden furnishings, Lavinia's guest, attired in her deep-blue coat and bonnet, looked as out of place inside the cottage as the carriage did parked outside of it. Lavinia was too surprised by this turn of events to know quite what to do. Who was this woman and why was she here?

The woman stood by the fire, holding her gloved hands over the flames, as she rubbed them, "There is nothing like a good fire on a winter's day, wouldn't you agree?"

"Yes, ma'am. I can make you a cup of tea. I do not have much, but I do have some bread."

"That won't be necessary," the woman said as she turned around to face Lavinia, "Come and sit down beside me – we have much to discuss."

"We do?" Lavinia asked as she sat on a low wooden stool, leaving the good chair for her guest.

"We do, my girl. Let me have a look at you," the older woman said as she leaned close to Lavinia. She touched Lavinia's chin and gently turned her face one way and then the next, peering closely at her. Lavinia was not sure why she was being studied, but she almost expected the woman to ask her to open her mouth, so she could see her teeth, like a plough horse at the market.

"You have my petite frame and my fine features. Those cheekbones you inherited from my son. Let me see... your hair is as dark as a raven and you have dark eyes – you must have got those from your mother... she was a beauty," the woman said as she held one of Lavinia's hands. "Your skin is fair. I see your mother did a good job of keeping you out of the sun – splendid."

Lavinia did not intend to be rude, but she was confused, "Ma'am, I do not mean to be impertinent, but I do not know whom I am addressing?"

"My poor dear Lavinia, you do not know me? I am your grandmother. I am Mrs Henrietta Talridge, but you may call me whatever pleases you."

"Grandmother?" Lavinia mouthed the word, unable to speak for a moment. Swallowing, she found her voice again, "I haven't a grandmother. I have no family."

"You do have family, my girl. You have *me*. Your father, God rest his soul, was my son, my only son. You are a Talridge, my dear."

"No, there must be some mistake – my name is Dean."

"Your mother's name was Dean. If you like you may keep it, but to me, you shall be a Talridge. You are all I have left of my dear son; you and I are family."

Lavinia was overwhelmed by the news and she slowly stood up. She needed a few minutes to collect her thoughts and to make sense of these events. She walked away from the fireside and paced the floor in the confined space.

She sighed. *This is impossible.*

"Forgive my rudeness, but this cannot be true. My mother told me my father was dead and that I had no-one but her," Lavinia replied, her voice cracking from the emotion she could barely conceal.

"My dear, why should you believe me? Here I am a woman you do not know, who has burst in on you at this terrible time of grief. You have been through so much. Sit down, and I will tell you the truth."

Lavinia sat down on her wooden stool beside the fire. She did not know what the truth was, but if there was even the slightest possibility that she may not be alone in the world, she was willing to hear it.

"How old are you?"

"I am not yet fourteen."

"You are practically a woman... Has it really been so long ago? Let me see, where should I start? I know; I will begin with my son, your father. As I have said, he was my only child. He was a handsome man and he enjoyed a good book and hunting. Your mother was the daughter of a couple who tended the sheep and cattle on my estate. She was a beauty, but you know that, don't you, my dear? My son fell in love with her, but they kept their love secret... I did not know about it. Yes, they kept their love hidden. I suppose he would have thought me too old-fashioned to accept a woman with no connections or family background as a wife, and I am ashamed to say he was right. I wanted my son to marry a woman who was accomplished in all things a lady ought to be. I wanted him to find a wife who could manage the household, entertain guests, and play music. I was blinded by my own ambitions for my son. I did not see... that he showed no interest in any of the eligible young women he met when we went to London for the season."

"You said my mother's parents lived on your estate... are they still alive?" Lavinia wanted to know.

Mrs Talridge shook her head slowly, "No my dear, they died a long time ago, I am sorry to say. They were a good sort of people, hardworking and useful. You would have been proud to know them. They raised your mother to be the same, to work hard for her living."

"And... If you do not mind me asking... was your son in love with my mother?"

"Yes, my son, your father, was in love with your mother. When we returned from London, he made secret plans to marry her. They decided to be wed at the end of the summer, but he, bless his soul, was killed crossing a stream, before they could marry. He was riding his favourite steed, an enormous chestnut if I remember correctly. My poor son fell from the saddle and broke his neck. He died instantly." the old woman said as she reached into the silken purse hanging from her wrist. Retrieving an embroidered handkerchief, she dabbed at her eyes.

"He did not suffer, did he?"

"No, my dear, he did not. I was overcome with grief, however... my husband, your grandfather, had died the year before. When I lost my son, it was more than I could bear. I retreated into a world of grief and despair. I did not want to eat or to leave my room in the morning. For many months, I was inconsolable. It was not until my maid brought me the news that a baby had been born on the estate... a baby that was born out of wedlock, that I had the slightest interest in anything or anyone. At first, I was shocked by the scandal. Who would have been so blatant in their sin to have a baby without the benefit of marriage? I discovered that it was your mother who had given birth... I went to see her that day. It was then that I discovered that my son had been in love with her and that they were planning to be wed. When she told me the news, I did not believe it, but her parents were insistent. They had never lied to me before, so I had no reason to doubt them. As I listened to their story, fantastic as it was, I recalled details about my son that suggested that they were telling the truth..." she looked deep into Lavinia's eyes. "When I held you in my arms, I knew that you were my granddaughter. I felt it in my heart."

"Why have I never met you?" Lavinia asked curiously.

"I do not wish to speak ill of the dead, but that is the fault of your mother, as equally as it is my own. I wanted to have a hand in raising you. I couldn't acknowledge you, of course. You were born out of wedlock... but I had plans for you. When you were of age, I was going to send you to school and give you an education, but your mother did not wish for me to interfere. You were her daughter and the only piece of my son that she had left. Oh, we fought about you bitterly! When she refused to accept my help, I threatened to take you away.

Your mother left soon after that and I did not see her again for many months. By then, she had been living on her own and making her own way in the world. She agreed to take money for your clothes and food, to keep you safe and warm, but she would not take a penny more. I promised I would respect her wishes. I would let her raise you but that when you were older and could make your own choices, I would send for you."

"I was born out of wedlock? My mother and father weren't married? That is not true, it cannot be. She told me she was married, and that my father died when I was a baby," Lavinia gasped.

"We won't tell anyone... No-one needs to know. They were going to be married and they had made plans to be wed. He intended to marry her; it was his wish. I decided long ago that when you were older, I would acknowledge you, and I would call you my granddaughter. I should have done it already... but my pride, my terrible pride, stood in the way."

Lavinia reached for the poker and stirred the embers of the dying fire. This morning, she had known who she was. This morning, she was Lavinia Dean, the daughter of a widowed seamstress. Now, she was Lavinia Dean, the granddaughter of a wealthy woman, who was seated across from her at the fireside, and she had been born out of wedlock. The shame of her birth crashed down on her as terribly as the grief she had felt at her mother's passing. She was nobody and she was a child of sin.

"Let the fire die. We have a long journey to be home in time for dinner," Mrs Talridge said as she stood up.

"*This* is my home," Lavinia answered.

"Not anymore. You are my granddaughter and you're coming with me."

"But... but... I do not want to leave Cotes Cross," Lavinia said, in a panic.

"You can return any time you like, my dear child. Come on, do not tarry. Gather your things," her grandmother rushed.

Lavinia understood that if she left, she would be leaving the only home, she had ever known. The last connection to her mother would be severed when she walked out the door. As badly as it pained her to leave the small cottage, she knew that she did not have a choice, so she slowly packed her clothes into a plain satchel. Before she said goodbye to the cottage, she also packed the wooden box from the mantle, a china case from her mother's bedside table, and her sewing box.

She was in agony as she closed the door for the last time. She did not want to forget her mother, nor the years they had spent in the little house. She vowed that she would never forget the happy memories of her mother singing to her as she sewed.

With fear in her heart, Lavinia sang a verse of her mother's favourite hymn, as she left the cottage forever.

...

End of the Reading Sample.

Books in the Same Series

The Wharton Series:

A Bride for the Viscount's Cold Son

The Duke of the Moors

An Orphan for the Duke

More Books by Audrey Ashwood:

Miss Honeyfield and the Dark Duke

The Cold Earl's Bride

Books by Audrey Ashwood & Rosie Wynter:

The Curtis Sisters Books 1-3:

To Love A Rogue

To Steal A Duke's Heart

To Romance A Scoundrel

Also available as Box Set:

The Curtis Sisters

The Author

Audrey Ashwood

Author of Clean Historical Romance

Audrey Ashwood hails from London, the city where she was born and raised. At a young age, she began diving into the world of literature, a world full of fairy tales and Prince Charmings. Writing came later – no longer was she a spectator of fantasies; she was now a creator of them.

In her books, the villains get their just desserts – her stories are known for happy and deserved endings. Love, of course, plays a major role, even if it's not the initial star of the show. With each written word, Audrey hopes to remind people that love transcends oceans and generations.

Don't miss out on exciting offers and new releases.

Sign up for her newsletter and the exclusive Reader's Circle: www.audreyashwood.com/releases

Legal Information

The Duke of the Moors;
A Regency Romance Novel
by Audrey Ashwood;

Published by:
ARP 5519, 1732 1st Ave #25519 New York, NY 10128
April 2019
Contact: info@allromancepublishing.com

2. Edition Paperback (Version 1.3); January 2nd, 2020

Image Rights:

© Novel Expression
© FairytaleDesign / Depositphotos.com

Made in the USA
Monee, IL
07 May 2020